Sant

Country Cottage Mystery #3

Addison Moore

and

Bellamy Bloom

Edited by Paige Maroney Smith
Cover by Lou Harper, Cover Affairs
Published by Hollis Thatcher Press, LTD.

Books by the Authors

Cozy Mysteries

Country Cottage Mysteries

Kittyzen's Arrest (Country Cottage Mysteries 1)

Dog Days of Murder (Country Cottage Mysteries 2)

Santa Claws Calamity (Country Cottage Mysteries 3)

Bow Wow Big House (Country Cottage Mysteries 4)

Murder Bites (Country Cottage Mysteries 5)

Murder in the Mix

Cutie Pies and Deadly Lies (Murder in the Mix 1)

Bobbing for Bodies (Murder in the Mix 2)

Pumpkin Spice Sacrifice (Murder in the Mix 3)

Gingerbread and Deadly Dread (Murder in the Mix 4)

Seven-Layer Slayer (Murder in the Mix 5)

Red Velvet Vengeance (Murder in the Mix 6)

Bloodbaths and Banana Cake (Murder in the Mix 7)

New York Cheesecake Chaos (Murder in the Mix 8)

Lethal Lemon Bars (Murder in the Mix 9)

Macaron Massacre (Murder in the Mix 10)

Wedding Cake Carnage (Murder in the Mix 11)

Donut Disaster (Murder in the Mix 12)

Toxic Apple Turnovers (Murder in the Mix 13)
Killer Cupcakes (Murder in the Mix 14)
Pumpkin Pie Parting (Murder in the Mix 15)
Yule Log Eulogy (Murder in the Mix 16)
Pancake Panic (Murder in the Mix 17)
Sugar Cookie Slaughter (Murder in the Mix 18)
Devil's Food Cake Doom (Murder in the Mix 19)

1

My name is Bizzy Baker, and I read minds. Not every mind, not every time, but it happens, and believe me when I say it's not all it's cracked up to be.

Like say now for instance.

My, my—Camila Ryder offers a dark smile as she takes me in—***aren't you and Jasper an adorable couple? Out and about on this December night, pretending to be a family.***

I shoot a side-glance at my newly minted boyfriend, Detective Jasper Wilder. He's six-foot-two, dark hair, has eyes the color of lightning bolts, and is a bit ornery around the edges. He commands the attention of every woman in all of Maine simply by being present in the state, and yet, for some reason, he's chosen me to spend his time with.

Lucky, lucky me.

Camila is Jasper's ex-girlfriend, who has since decided that she wants him back. And that potshot about having a family has everything to do with the fact I'm pushing a stroller specially designed to house my sweet kitten, Fish.

As soon as I started in on how excited I was to see the Christmas lights on Candy Cane Lane this year, Fish begged to join me, and I wasn't about to deny her a night of illuminated holiday fun.

And yes, I can read an animal's mind as well as a human's—and as far as I'm concerned, animals have nicer things to say.

Sherlock lets out a sharp bark as if in agreement.

Sherlock Bones is a red freckled mixed breed that Jasper adopted before we met. Sherlock is a sweetheart of a pooch, and he and Fish get along famously, *mostly*.

The sound of a bell chiming across the street demands our attention as a group of carolers, complete in Dickens' era costumes, starts off with a harmonizing tune before they break out into a cheery rendition of "We Wish You a Merry Christmas."

Next to the cheery carolers is a stand with an oversized sign that reads *Christmas Treats*! It has a menu written in large print that boasts of hot cocoa, eggnog, and frosted sugar cookies—the three basic food groups this time of year. And that's exactly where Jasper and I were headed before we bumped into the ghost of girlfriends past.

It's the official opening night of Candy Cane Lane, an area of residential houses on the west end of Cider Cove where they go all out with Christmas decorations. Each home selects a theme and somehow works Christmas into it, and everyone in Cider Cove comes out to cast their vote for their favorite over-the-top holiday display. And that's exactly what we're doing tonight. Each home has a different motif. There's an adorable display featuring the Peanuts characters, others have a traditional snowman, some celebrate the Grinch, and others hold true to the meaning of the season with a simple nativity.

Visiting Candy Cane Lane is something I've done since I was a child. And each year I look forward to coming here and seeing the decorated houses as well as the famed oak trees that line the streets in these neighborhoods. The overgrown oaks are planted next to the sidewalk and go on in a line as far as the eye can see. Each oak is strung up with white twinkle lights, illuminating all of Candy Cane Lane with the enchanted appeal of a winter wonderland. As a whole, it creates a magical aura only this season can bring.

But it's the houses that steal the show.

Two of the houses have really turned the Christmas spirit on high volume this year, and that would be the

Bronsons' and the Brooks' homes, which are both located directly across the street from one another. And oddly, both homes have decided to go with the very same North Pole theme with a dedicated throne for Santa. Each of the houses is buzzing with bodies as the crowds press in trying to get a look at the thousands of lights, the shiny wrapped gifts that sit under the enormous well-decorated—and well-illuminated—evergreen trees erected on their front lawns. There are lines snaking around each of their driveways as children wait eagerly to speak with the head elf himself and yet both Santas seem to be suspiciously away from their thrones at the moment.

But just prior to the great Santa disappearance, it's been confusing and delightful for all the little kids here to say the least. They kept crossing the street with their parents, making sure to ask both of the men in red suits for gifts as to not accidently whisper their sincerest desire to the phony of the two.

"Camila." Jasper takes a breath and sags as he says her name. I snap to, momentarily forgetting all about her evil presence. *Evil* might sound a bit harsh, but it's not much of a stretch. "Enjoying the lights?"

"That I am." She warms her arms with her hands. Camila is a stunning beauty with long, dark, wavy hair and cutting features that could easily have earned her millions as a supermodel. But she's as cunning as she is beautiful. Not only is she gunning to land Jasper back by her side, but she's somehow discovered that I'm able to read minds.

You see, when Camila cheated on Jasper with his best friend, Deputy Leo Granger, way back when, she had somehow figured out that Leo, too, could pry into people's most intimate thoughts. So naturally when she saw both Leo and me communicating without the effort of our lips, she put two and two mind readers together. Now she's threatened me with all sorts of horrible things in an effort to get me to dump Jasper so she can have him back.

As if.

I shake my head at the thought. There is no way I'm going down without a fight. Camila can get a bullhorn and shout out the fact I can read minds to the world, but I'll deny it until I'm blue in the face. Despite her best adolescent efforts, she can't scare me.

Okay—fine. She scares me just a little. But she can't scare me much.

"So Bizzy"— Camila leans in, that manufactured grin of hers ever-expanding—"I took a look at the activities board for the month, and it seems I've settled in the right locale. The Country Cottage Inn is the place to be in December."

I can't help but frown.

It's true. Camila is taking up residence at the Country Cottage Inn where I'm currently the manager. The inn itself is a massive structure that mirrors a colonial era mansion. And in addition to the inn itself, we rent over thirty cottages that are scattered across the grounds. Both Jasper and I happen to each live in our own cottages, and as fate would have it, we're next-door neighbors. Jasper fled to Cider Cove after Camila sliced his heart open and ate it.

And here she is, hungry for the rest of him.

I look right at her and force a smile. ***You're not getting another bite.***

"That's right." I raise my voice a notch over the carolers and over all holiday revelry as the crowds start to balloon from seemingly nowhere. "We'll have an activity every few days—crafts and cooking demonstrations, and there will be a benefit the Sunday night before Christmas Eve—the Let It Snow Ball. All proceeds collected from the ticket sales and silent auction will go directly to help provide Christmas meals for families in need."

"Oh, wow." Camila chortles as she looks to Jasper. "You really found the jewel in the bunch with this one, haven't you?" She offers me a mocking nod. "You're very altruistic, Bizzy. I can see why you've captured Jasper's heart." She tightens her smile as she looks to me. ***Don't blink, Bizzy. He'll be mine before you know it.*** "Any other events I should be aware of? I'm new to Cider Cove. This will be my very first Christmas here."

And hopefully last.

Jasper threads his fingers with mine and gives my hand a gentle squeeze. ***Don't do it, Bizzy. Whatever you do, don't invite her to Christmas Eve dinner. I can feel her angling for something. Come to think of it, it's probably me.***

A dull laugh warms in my chest at his thoughts. Jasper has no idea I can read his mind—and thankfully so. I'm not sure what would become of us if he did.

I clear my throat as I look to Camila. "That's all that I know of." I push Fish's stroller along a few inches, hoping Camila will take the hint. "Enjoy the neighborhood. I'm sure we'll see you around." Unfortunately.

"You'll both see me," she practically sings as the two of us start off down the street. "I'm the coordinator for your mother's wedding, Jasper."

We both stop cold in our tracks as an icy wind cuts right through our winter coats.

Jasper gives a sly look back. "She's gone." He gives a long blink. "Why did she have to remind us of that looming disaster?"

"Because *she's* a looming disaster."

Sherlock barks. ***That's right, Bizzy. That woman has never been kind to me. Did you see her openly refuse to acknowledge me? She didn't even have a sliver of bacon in her pocket to greet me the way you do.*** He nuzzles his forehead to my knee and I offer him a quick pat on the head.

Jasper gives a mournful laugh. "She is a disaster. One I thought I would be able to avoid. Is there any way you could evict her from the inn?"

"Not that I know of. Is there any way you can arrest her?" I'm only half-teasing. Jasper is the lead homicide detective down at the Seaview Sheriff's Department, and I wouldn't be opposed to him putting his badge to good use.

An all too familiar couple bustles in this direction and my stomach churns. Just look at these two, holding hands, grinning like lunatics at one another as if they were genuinely in love.

A hard groan comes from me. "I think Camila is the least of our troubles. Don't look now, but there's a looming disaster at six o'clock."

Jasper cranes his neck past the crowd of bundled bodies, and his eyes enlarge once he sees the heresy.

A few months back, his mother, Gwyneth Wilder, a divorcee, and my father, Nathan Baker, the *king* of divorces—with more marital dissolutions under his belt than the annals of history can number—collided like two battleships in the night set on a collision course for calamity. And after about three solid weeks of partial interactions, half-hearted hellos, and perhaps one or two instances where they were in the same place at the same time for under thirty minutes, they announced that they would be tying the knot this Christmas Eve.

I predict it's going to be less of a celebratory event and more like an Irish wake. In other words, a night steeped in deep regret and mourning—at least for Jasper and me.

"Mom." Jasper pulls the woman who brought him into this world in for a quick embrace, and I do the same with my father. "It's nice to see you getting out and enjoying the season." Jasper looks to my father. "Nathan, it's good to see you, too. My mother isn't typically a fan of these kinds of events."

Of course, she's not. Good tidings and joy aren't typically on the top of the list for your average Scrooge.

A twinge of remorse blips through me. I'm not trying to disparage her. It's just that I sort of can't help it. Gwyneth Wilder made it clear to me when we met that I wasn't good enough for her son. In fact, she worked her hardest to reconnect Jasper with his ex, the aforementioned Camila. I suppose that's what the wedding coordinator stunt is about, too. At least in part. I'm guessing Camila came up with that breakup brainstorm—the aforementioned breakup just so happens to feature Jasper and me.

"Bizzy Bizzy, how's it going, kid?" Dad gives my ear a playful tug before he does a double take at the stroller. "What's this? I haven't been away nine whole months, have I?" He takes a peek inside the mesh net keeping Fish from running wild into the streets. "I'm too young and good looking to be a grandpa."

"You're a grandpa, all right," I say. "And your granddaughter has pointed ears and a furry tail."

The four of us share a warm laugh on my playful father's behalf. Dad has always had an irresistible boyish quality about him. And that's exactly how he's gotten away with marrying and divorcing so many women without his head—or other far more southern anatomical features—ending up on the chopping block.

He's notorious for all of his exes loving him post their amicable dissolutions. I don't think there's been a soul who hasn't been susceptible to my father's charm. Even Gwyneth's well-tarnished soul has succumbed to his snake charmer-like advances. Which explains a lot, considering.

"It's just Fish, Dad," I say, unzipping the netting a few inches so he can take a peek. "And yes, you are very much a grandfather to her. She's just as sweet as a human, if not sweeter."

Fish yowls. ***Thanks for the endorsement, Bizzy. You're not going to have one of those human babies with Jasper, are you? I've seen the destruction they're capable of. And they're not trained to squat and bury. They do their business right in their pants! I'm not sure the cottage would be big enough for a creature like that.***

A small laugh trembles from me.

A baby with Jasper—now there's a thought.

Dad coos and scratches at the netting before straightening again.

Dad and I share the same dark, wavy hair. Mine touches just past my shoulders, and he wears his short and thick like a carpet. We also happen to share the same icy blue eyes, although his seem to be backlit at the moment.

"Jasper"—Dad takes a deep breath, expanding his chest the size of a door—"Bizzy." He nods my way as if signaling things just took a turn for the serious. "Gwynie and I would like to invite you both to Maximus' next week for dinner." Maximus is a snazzy restaurant out in Seaview owned by Jasper's brother who happens to share the moniker of his well-beloved eatery. Another odd but fun fact? Max is my mother's current hot-to-trot boyfriend. "Of course, we're inviting *all* of our children so we can get to know one another a little better." ***And hopefully by the time this wedding rolls around, her kids won't want to slaughter me.***

I wrinkle my nose at my dear old dad.

I'm about to tell him that I think he and *Gwynie* should get to know one another—for like a year—or a decade—maybe a millennium or two, when the sound of two men arguing garners our attention. We collectively look to our left and our mouths fall open at what we see.

Two men in jolly red suits, cheesy white scraggly wigs, and cumbersome hats are shouting obscenities while threatening one another at top volume.

"Good Lord"—I whisper to Jasper—"it's Santa versus Santa."

Jasper hands me Sherlock's leash. "I'd better get over there before this gets ugly."

"Me too," Dad says as they take off in a flash.

Two salty versions of Santa Claus have landed in Cider Cove, and they're about to throw punches.

Something tells me we might be in store for the scariest merriest Christmas of them all.

2

A frosty breeze whips through the neighborhood, causing the twinkle lights up above to rattle like skeletons as the oaks give a violent shudder.

Candy Cane Lane is alive with holiday hungry crowds as the streets grow thick with bodies. Cars drive bumper to bumper as kids press their noses to the windows, trying to take in all of the colorful glory this celebratory season has to offer.

I'm huddled in my thickest winter coat on the sidewalk just outside of Lincoln Brooks' house, a fancy two-story with a colonial feel that currently looks as if the Christmas fairy hit it hard with her candy cane-shaped wand. The entire place is lit up from the roof, the eaves, the columns, and around the door and windows. Clearly, there are more than enough lumens happening here to light up all of Cider Cove.

Honest to goodness, the house glows like its very own moon. And then, there are the miles of cotton batting laid across the front lawn with tiny blue lights illuminated from underneath to give it the appeal of fresh fallen snow. It's a beautiful sight and makes me wish the temperatures would drop just a notch or two tonight so we can have the real icy deal. But the most interesting component is the fact the lights are set to music—rather loud music that causes both the lights and the neighborhood to pulsate like a seizure as it pounds relentlessly into the night.

But that's not currently the spectacle that's grabbing everyone's attention. It's the two dueling Santas who look ready to escalate from a war of words to a war of knuckles and perhaps a knee to the groin.

Jasper and Dad fly up the lawn, padded with fake snow, in an effort to break up the not-so-jolly elf showdown, but the situation only seems to grow more volatile.

A woman pops between the two men in their oversized red suits, and I lean in and squint because I'd swear on all the Christmas gifts I've already charged to my credit card I recognize that woman as my very own mother.

"*Bizzy*!" a familiar voice croaks from behind and I turn to find Georgie running up with her gray hair wild and loose, her body wrapped in some sort of a coat that's pieced together from every colorful strip of fabric known to man.

Georgie Conner is one of my father's many ex-mothers-in-law. But unlike the others, Georgie was mildly forgotten and left behind by her daughter. I like to tease that I got Georgie in the divorce. She happens to rent out a cottage that sits right behind the inn where she keeps busy by crushing glass for her extensive mosaic projects.

"*Bizzy*." She grips me by the shoulders. "Santa One and Santa Two are about to knock each other's teeth out! We can't let the kids see this madness. They'll grow up to be brute beasts who'll come to blows over anything. All of humanity will be ruined if we let this happen! *Ruined*, I tell you!" She jostles me so hard my necklace bounces over my chest. "We need to *do* something!"

"You're right," I say, giving her Sherlock's leash while placing her other hand on Fish's stroller. "Mind these two. I'll be right back."

I race up the lawn, only to find my mother trying her best to sandwich herself between the battling bloated men in cheap polyester suits.

"*Ree Baker*," I snip as I pluck my mother from the midst of the feuding Saint Nicks.

Mom's sandy blonde hair is neatly feathered back and her makeup is impeccably done, right down to her perfectly adhered false eyelashes. My mother always looks great no matter what age she bypasses like a seasoned pro. She has a timeless sense of style, if that time was circa 1981. Not that there's anything wrong with that. She's been sporting the well-dressed preppy look for as long as I can remember and has kept her iconic feathered hair trimmed just long enough to dust her shoulders as if it weren't capable of growing another inch.

"Mother?" I yank her back a few paces away from the melee as another woman takes her place between the two overheated hotheads. "Have you lost your mind?"

"Please." She frees her wrist from my stranglehold and rubs it. "It's not me who's lost my mind. It's Lincoln and Dexter." She points to the two men currently being restrained by Jasper and my father.

"That's Lincoln Brooks and Dexter Bronson?" I squint up at the men with their sagging pants and wayward false beards. "Hey? Didn't you date Lincoln once or twice?"

"Yup." She leans in my way. "And that's Mary Beth between them." She nods up at a woman with short black hair, and her red glossy lips are twisted in every direction at once as she shouts to the belligerent Santas between her.

"She used to be married to Lincoln eons ago. But she's been married to Dexter for years now."

"Oh, wow. I didn't realize she was married to Lincoln. How weird is that? I mean, they live across the street from one another." I glance over to the house in question across the street lit up with colorful lights. A giant blowup of an entire snowman family sits crooked to the side, and in the center of the lawn is an enormous golden throne with red velvet padding, temporarily abandoned due to the Christmas chaos underway.

Mom waves it off. "It's not that weird. That was originally the Brooks' house, but Mary Beth got it in the divorce. And well, Lincoln said he liked the neighborhood so much he bought the only house available at the time." She shrugs. "Directly across the street."

"That must make for interesting block parties. Hey? Did Lincoln and Mary Beth have any kids together?"

"No, Brooks doesn't have any. Dexter and Mary Beth have three. Two boys and a girl."

"I could never live across the street from my ex." I shudder at the thought and Mom laughs.

"Bizzy, you don't have any serious exes."

"I do, too," I'm quick to contest. "I was married once."

She's right back to laughing. "For less than a day to your best friend's brother. And you have Vegas and bad rum to blame for it. It took *your* brother longer to untangle you from the mess than it did for you to enjoy it."

"Well, I *didn't* enjoy it." True as gospel. "I spent my wedding night with my head in the toilet."

"You just described my marriage to your father perfectly." Mom threads her arm through mine as she leads me back to the two men in Santa suits. They're holding their pointed hats and curly beards in one hand, and with the other they seem to be toasting one another with a cup of eggnog.

"What's this?" Mom balks with a laugh in her throat. "Please tell me it's a truce and not a new way to torment one another."

A tall blonde honks out a laugh. "It's nothing a little good old-fashioned spiked eggnog can't fix." She gives a hard wink our way, and I can't help but notice the layers of caked foundation on her face, crusting up like sedimented strata. Her long, thick lashes look as if she's doubled or tripled the falsies, her lips are painted a frosty shade of pink, and her hair is pulled back into a long ponytail that touches all the way down to her waist.

She looks as if she has ten years on me, so I'm guessing mid-thirties. She's dressed in an adorable, yet slightly revealing, Mrs. Claus outfit—the skirt of which hardly crests her tush—and she's paired the look with thigh-high red patent leather boots that scream they're better suited for a street corner in the North Pole rather than Santa Central.

She gives a little wave to my mother and me. "I'm Trixie Jolly-Golightly, Lincoln's plus one." She gives a hearty wink our way, and if I didn't know she had on false lashes, I'd swear on all that was holy she has accidentally glued a couple of dead moths to her lids.

Mom leans in my way. "Trixie Jolly-Golightly? Do you think that's her stage name?"

I make a face at the woman who bore me. For some reason, my mother landed on this planet without a filter on her mouth. Having her around mixed company has always been a lot like a box of chatty chocolates. You never know what you're going to get, and yet every bite seems to be an unwanted cherry royal pain in the rear.

Thankfully, the talking ponytail is sidetracked with another conversation by a thinner girl, pretty in a plain sort of way with her hair in a bun and a pair of large tortoise-rimmed glasses sitting on the edge of her nose. And next to the two of them is a man standing slumped, his hands buried in his pockets as he glares over at the surly Santas before us.

Mary Beth appears with a tray full of cups brimming with the delicious holiday concoction.

"Eggnog for everyone!" she sings. "Our stand is just across the street. It's cash only but, in an effort to bestow goodwill upon our neighbors, we're willing to part with a little of the holiday favorite in order to mend a few fences."

I'll make sure to squeeze it out of Lincoln sooner than later. Once I wrap my hands around his proverbial neck, he won't know what hit him.

Squeeze it? I don't know what *it* is, but I'm not looking forward to the live demonstration.

She holds the tray out, and everyone in the vicinity is quick to snap one up. Jasper hands one to both my mother and me.

It sounds as if Mary Beth and Lincoln still have a little bad blood between them. A lot of bad blood if you count Dexter in the mix.

"How was that for a little Christmas cheer?" Jasper hoists his cup our way as if he were toasting us.

"Jasper"—Mom toasts him with her cup as well—"thank you for stepping up like the man you are. Let me introduce you to the clowns you were spared from arresting. Lincoln, Dexter?" she calls out and the two red-faced Santas head on over.

Lincoln Brooks is a stockier man by nature, with a slanted forehead, heavy chin, and eyes that always look as if they're laughing at you. I wasn't too thrilled while he and my mother were dating. Despite the fact Lincoln is a real estate investor, and my mother was a very successful realtor, it just didn't seem like a natural pairing.

And Dexter is a thinner version of Lincoln, with the same thick chin and slanted forehead, albeit younger than Lincoln by about ten years. It's clear Mary Beth has a type.

Mom leans their way. "This is Jasper Wilder, Bizzy's new boyfriend." She practically whispers that last part to Lincoln as if they've already discussed my previous less than savory pairings.

"Nice to meet you," both Jasper and I chime in unison.

Dexter nods. "Likewise." He frowns over at us. "Now, be honest, which house do you think will take home the Candy Cane Lane People's Choice Award this year? This pile of fake snow and that splinter-inducing nightmare he calls a throne or that delightful winter wonderland across the street? A genuine gilded throne that sits proud in the center of the yard with plush red velvet backing—*and* a real live reindeer as a sidekick?" ***Anyone with two working eyeballs knows class when they see it. And after what I have planned, they'll know Lincoln has been rigging these spectacles to swing his way for years. The old coot won't know what hit him—or should I say, who?***

I blink back. It's almost the same threat Mary Beth just issued. Poor Lincoln. He *really* won't know what hit him.

Lincoln belts out a belligerent belly laugh. "The only reason your house looks half as good as it does, Dex, is because you can't come up with a single original idea. You and Mary Beth have been stealing my concepts for years."

Mom, Jasper, and I crane our necks to get a better look across the street, and sure enough there seems to be some large land mammal gnawing on the flowerbed.

I clear my throat. "Well, that alone says something. After all, they say imitation is the sincerest form of flattery."

Dexter rocks back in his oversized boots. "We don't imitate." He looks over to Lincoln, his chest puffing up with pride. "And we don't do second class. We're not into tasteless cheap renditions of the real thing." He gives a sly glance toward Trixie as she breaks out into a howl of laughter while nudging at the girl with the bun. She seems blissfully oblivious that the potshot was geared toward her.

"Hey"—Lincoln gives Dexter a quick shove to the chest—"you lay off my girl. You don't see me badmouthing your *secondhand* wife, do you?"

"Whoa." Jasper holds out an arm. "Leave the ladies out of it. This is a family event."

"There are kids here," I'm quick to point out because neither of the cranky Kringles really seems to notice.

Lincoln laughs openly at Dexter. "You do realize I won the last three years in a row." He looks our way. ***And I happen to know I'm about to win again***. "This is just sour grapes—or should I say, sour eggnog?" He takes another sip from his cup and makes a face. "I don't know how you stay in business peddling this poison. But I'll knock it down, just like I'm going to knock you down another notch and score the W for a fourth year in a row." He chugs the eggnog before crushing the cup against his forehead. "How do you like that?" He winces as if he doesn't care for the taste of it.

I think it tastes great. In fact, I'm about to knock back the rest of my own just as Mary Beth steps in with a basket of adorable fuzzy kittens. They both look identical with their matching same long gray hair and glowing green eyes, and suddenly I have a craving to snuggle.

"*Kittens*!" Georgie howls as she runs on over with Sherlock in tow and Fish in her arms. I knew Georgie wouldn't get behind the idea of keeping Fish locked up in a glorified tent for the night, and a small part of me is glad about it. "Oh! Can we keep them, Bizzy? Can we? The inn is so barren with just the one kitten running amuck." She lands a kiss to Fish's furry forehead.

My sweet cat shudders as she looks my way. ***Don't even think about it, Bizzy. I'm the head feline at the inn—the only feline. As it should be. It's bad enough we have Sherlock thinking he's a bona fide greeter now. How many beasts can one inn take before it becomes too beastly, for beasts' sake? And I can't share my bed. I absolutely refuse. You know I'm very particular about pet hair getting on my blanket.***

I roll my eyes at that one. Fish hasn't slept a single night in the cat bed I bought for her. She happily sleeps in *my* bed. Come to think of it, that may be the bed she's referring to.

Sherlock licks his lips as he looks to the basket of cuteness. ***They look delicious, Bizzy. Can we wrap them in bacon? They're so small, I bet I can eat them in three solid bites.***

Good grief. I all but chuckle at that one.

"Georgie," I say. "I don't think Mary Beth is giving these precious dumplings away."

Mary Beth blinks back.

There's a pixie quality about her, and somewhat of a nasty streak that you can see in her beady eyes all at the same time.

She grunts, "*Please* take these furballs off my hands. My kids are allergic, and I can't stand the thought of hairballs. My sister had a litter, and I snapped up two thinking they'd be a good lure to get people to the snack stand. And let me tell you, I think I should name them Money and Bags." She brays out a laugh, and both my mother and I recoil at the very same time. Is that a real laugh? Or is she doing her best impersonation of that donkey from Bethlehem that lived all those years ago on that holy silent night?

Georgie produces a dollar bill from out of nowhere and wags it in the air. "Sold to the highest bidder! We'll take 'em!"

Georgie holds Fish up to the fuzzy gray twins trying their best to cower behind one another.

"Oh, it's perfect timing, Bizzy," Georgie bleats. "Don't you have an appointment at the v-e-t tomorrow to get Fish and Sherlock f-i-x-e-d? We can take these two cuties along for the ride and get them checked out."

The hair rises on Fish's back. ***Why is she cutting her words down to letters? What is this appointment business?***

Sherlock lets out a little bark. ***Does the appointment involve bacon? I'm sensing this is a solid no.***

I'm not sure how, but the animals always seem to understand one another through no more than a growl or whimper.

Lincoln staggers a few steps forward and nearly knocks the basket right out of Mary Beth's hand and the entire lot of us gasps.

Dexter pulls him back with a violent yank. "Watch where you're going, old man."

"Who are you calling old?" Lincoln pulls Dexter in by the shirt and lets out a riotous moan in the process.

Jasper gets between them this time just as Dad runs over once again, as well as the man who was standing near Trixie.

"Let go." Dexter takes a full step back. "If Lincoln wants to nail me over the face, I say be my guest. Go ahead, Linc. Hit me with your best shot." He points to his chin, his chest puffed out as he dares him to do it. "Right *here*."

Lincoln doesn't miss a beat. He swings—but misses by a mile. He staggers over a few feet, gripping at his stomach and letting out another riotous moan. Lincoln spins and writhes as he wraps his hands around his neck, and he seems to be struggling for air.

Someone in the crowd screams. And before Jasper can pull out his phone to call for help, Lincoln lands facedown in the fake snow right in front of that throne he erected in his front yard.

Jasper runs over and kneels next to him, checking his pulse at the neck. He looks my way and shakes his head ever so slightly.

Lincoln Brooks won't have to worry about who will win the Candy Cane Lane Christmas decorating contest. In fact, he's decorated his house for the very last time.

Lincoln Brooks is dead.

3

"He's dead!" Trixie Jolly-Golightly wails into the night just as a crowd rushes over in haste—and among them is an entire throng of morbidly curious children.

Mom groans, "We need to get these kids out of here." Instinctively, she begins herding them away. My mother may have a rock-hard exterior, but she's a nurturer through and through.

"I'll help," Gwyneth says as she nabs the nearest little boy by his ear.

Something tells me that's a tried-and-true move on her part as well.

"I'm in." Dad claps his hands. "Come on, Georgie. Let's get these kids moving in another direction. No one's got a voice like you do. Put it to good use."

Georgie hands me Sherlock's leash and lets out an ear-splitting whistle. "If you're under eighteen, they're giving away free chocolate brownies down the street! Last one there has to pick up the reindeer droppings!" She takes off with Fish in tow.

Let's just hope that chocolate brownies and reindeer droppings are not one in the same.

Half the crowd disappears in a blur.

Poor kids. Not only were they faced with a dead Santa, but there's the very real prospect of a letdown of the chocolate variety.

The roar of a siren heads in this direction, and Trixie begins to wail right alongside it.

Mary Beth makes a retching noise as if she were about to be sick, and instinctively I take the basket brimming with two adorable kittens from her.

"Keep them," she shrieks. "The last thing I need is to break out in hives. I need to get back to the snack stand before it's pillaged of its loot." She warms her arms with her hands aggressively as if those hives were already taking effect, and my mouth falls open as I look at her.

Lincoln Brooks, the man she was once married to, is lying on the ground, dead as a doornail, and all she seems to care about are a couple of harmless hives. But then, everyone handles grief differently, I suppose, and to be truthful, she hasn't had time to process any of this. None of us have.

An ambulance pulls up, and as soon as Jasper briefs the EMTs, he heads my way.

"Bizzy." He does a quick glance around as Sherlock does his best to jump up on him. "Are you okay?" He pulls me in for a quick embrace and lifts the kittens in an effort to keep them from spilling out of the basket.

Sherlock barks as if to ask the same question.

"Yes." I pull back. "Do we know what happened?"

His gray eyes bear into mine. "It could have been a run-of-the-mill heart attack."

I tip my head to the side. "It could have been. But we both saw the way he was staggering around, clutching at his throat. Jasper, I think he might have been poisoned."

Sherlock tugs at the leash. ***Poisoned? I think we'd better find Fish and leave. Do you know where they don't serve poison? The Country Cottage Café. I suggest we all head there now. Georgie says they have gingerbread whoopie pies in the kitchen. I bet they taste like bacon.***

Before I can say a word, a hand latches onto my arm and spins me around until I'm staring right in the face of Mayor Mack Woods.

"My goodness, Bizzy. It's like you attract the dead these days." Mackenzie Woods is as cold-hearted as she is beautiful. I should know—we grew up together. She was one of my best friends right up until she pushed me into a whiskey barrel and held me under for the fun of it. That was middle school, so being the naïve girl I was, I forgave her.

Four things came from that horrible day. I grew terrified of submerging myself in any body of water. I acquired a fear of confined spaces. It initiated my general distrust of Mack Woods. And last, but never least, I gained the ability to pry into other people's minds. Come to find out, this strange gift I somehow acquired is called transmundane, further classified as telesensual. Simply put—I can now read minds, and I have Mack's whiskey barrel attack to thank for it. Of course, our friendship waned on until high school where she saw fit to steal every boyfriend I dared to have. And now she's the mayor of Cider Cove, just like her father and grandfather were before her. Go figure.

But judging by the fact Deputy Leo Granger is strapped to her side, I don't think that whole boyfriend stealing thing is going to be a problem anymore. At least I hope not.

Leo steps up. ***What's going on, Bizzy? Was it a homicide?***

Leo is classically tall, dark-haired, olive skinned, and handsome. He has dark, mysterious eyes and has a knowing smile that is constantly curving on his lips. It's just Leo and Georgie who know about my gift to read minds—and, of course, Camila, but I'm slow to count her on that list. She's a dangerous addition, to say the least.

Leo Granger. I all but growl it out in my mind. ***I have one serious bone to pick with you. And I find it rather convenient that you've been persona non grata since Halloween. Right about the same time that piranha you unleashed into the wild threatened me. Camila knows that you can read minds, and she knows that I can do it, too. And don't think she's above threatening me. She's already done it!***

His eyes expand to the size of silver dollars. ***Don't panic, Bizzy. We'll talk. Soon.***

Too late. I take a moment to glare at him. ***I'm plenty panicked.***

Jasper's chest expands. "Leo, Mayor Mack." ***Typical Leo. He's checking out Bizzy right in front of his date. Of course, he doesn't care that I'm here. Trying to steal my woman is par for the course with him. Good thing Bizzy is glaring at him. Maybe he'll get the message.***

Jasper continues, "The neighbor who owns this house passed away. We're not sure if it was natural causes or not, but I'll open an investigation if the coroner's report warrants it."

"Jasper," I whisper. "If Lincoln was murdered, we should start the investigation now."

Mack lets out a dark chuckle. "Don't worry, Detective Wilder. Bizzy has always lived up to her nickname. She is, in fact, a busybody. She's not trying to usurp your authority and emasculate you in the traditional sense. Unless, of course, time has hardened her and she's trying to do exactly that." ***I hope he dumps her by midnight***. Her lips pull back with a satisfied smile.

Leo raises a brow in my direction. ***Don't worry, Bizzy. He's not dumping you. Not by a long shot. He's too far gone. Way more than he ever was with Camila. Trust me. He plans on taking you to the finish line.***

Finish line? Okay, I'll admit, Leo has just stroked my ego. I'd like nothing more than to believe that Jasper is taken by me far more than he was with Camila.

Leo nods my way. ***That's right. We're talking marriage.***

My lips part before rounding out into a smile.

"Bizzy?" Jasper leans in. ***Why is she smiling at Leo like that? Don't tell me she's falling for the guy. I'm not sure my ego can take it.***

"Oh." My fingers float to my lips. "I just realized I was holding these precious little angels." I hold out the basket brimming with two frightened, yet impossibly adorable, fuzzy kittens. "Come here, you two." I land the basket down and scoop them up into my arms. "My goodness, you are lighter than air." I press a kiss to each of their feather soft foreheads.

Here we go, says the smaller one on the right. ***I bet she'll shove us in the closet all night like the last one.***

The slightly taller, darker of the two mewls. ***I believe they called it the garage. We were left in the trunk of the car. We're lucky we survived the night, I tell you.***

I gasp at the thought.

An entire barrage of sheriff's deputies take over the lawn, and both Jasper and Leo excuse themselves.

Mack steps in. "Who did this?" she hisses my way before gasping for air. "Oh my goodness, did you do this? Bizzy, are you a serial killer?" Her mouth widens into a smile as if this somehow pleased her on some level. "Cider Cove's very own little Bizzy Borden. Who would have thought it? Let me guess. You're trying to drum up business for that tired little inn of yours?"

Camila strides up with her hand over her throat as if I were about to slaughter her next. Not that I'm a serial killer, but with these two in front of me, it's a tempting proposition.

"What's happening?" Camila snarls. "Why is the sheriff's department here?" Her eyes enlarge at something in the street. "Why is the *coroner* here?"

"Ask Mayor Woods," I say, trotting off toward the scene of the crime, and I do believe there was one. Lincoln Brooks was perfectly fine until he took a sip of Mary Beth's eggnog.

A horrible thought comes to me as I scour the crowd for the curious couple, and sure enough I find both Mary Beth and her ornery husband, Dexter, holding one another while staring at Lincoln's deceased body on the ground.

My feet carry me in their direction before I can protest.

"I'm sorry about your neighbor." I shrug.

Mary Beth squints over at me. There's a dangerous gleam in her eyes, and it sends a chill up my spine.

I'm not sorry in the least. She gives a dark smile.

"Yes, well. I'm sure we'll be fine."

Dexter expands his chest, and the stubble on his cheeks reflects blue and red as the lights on the deputies' cruisers liven the night with a seizure of color.

"Like Mary Beth said, we'll be fine." He stiffens his resolve. ***And for once, I'll get a little sleep around here. I should have taken care of him years ago.***

My mouth falls open.

Did Dexter Bronson just confess?

Dexter nods just past me. "If you really want to offer someone a little condolence, I'd head over to Trixie. All those waterworks and yammering, it almost looks real." ***But then, that's what he paid her for. Making it look real.***

I tighten my hold over the sweet kittens in my arms. Sherlock sniffs around the wig dangling from Dexter's hand.

I smell death, Bizzy. Have Jasper arrest him so we can get back to the cottage and wrap those cats in bacon. His long pink tongue laps his mouth.

"I think I will go offer her my condolences. Have a good night," I say to the two of them before making a beeline for Trixie.

By the time I arrive, she's not alone. The homely looking girl with a bun is rubbing her back, and the man who was slouched over glaring at Lincoln a few minutes ago is standing off to the side—still glaring at Lincoln as if he owed him money, or a vital organ.

"I'm sorry for your loss," I say to the blonde currently lost in hysterics. You could set an opera to the roller coaster-like aria streaming from her mouth. I've never seen anyone grieve like this. With her long blonde ponytail whipping from side to side, her pink glossy lips set in a perfect O, it all looks rather cartoonish in nature.

Trixie stops her prolonged howls just enough to catch her breath.

She looks my way and lowers her lids. "That man was everything to me." It comes out breathy and forced, like bad acting, and I'm betting it is.

Her eyes flit to her purse, and she peers inside a moment. ***I need a cigarette right about now. As soon as I get in that house, I'm popping the champagne—in a bubble bath, of course. All this vocalizing is straining muscles I didn't even know I had.***

Trixie squints out a short-lived smile my way. "If you'll all excuse me, I think I'll go inside now. All these flashing lights are giving me a headache." ***And more of a reason to celebrate.*** She glances over at Lincoln just as they pull a sheet up over him. ***Goodnight, you old coot.***

Maybe now you'll have a little peace at last. I know I will.

She takes off and I blow out a quick breath.

It doesn't seem she was Lincoln's biggest fan. And ironically, she was the person seemingly closest to him.

I shrug over at the girl with a bun before holding out a hand to her. "I'm Bizzy Baker. I run the Country Cottage Inn."

"Julia Hart. I'm Lincoln's secretary." She winces. "Or I guess I was." She shudders. "I don't think I'll ever get used to saying that."

"I'm sorry. I guess you lost both a friend and a job. That's just terrible."

She shrugs as she reaches over and offers each of the sweet kittens in my arms a quick pat to the head. "I'm not too worried about it. I've got a small nest egg. I suppose there's another real estate investor who might need some side help, or I'll apply for an office job of some sort. I don't really have any ties to Cider Cove. I just moved here a few months back. I really like it, though. I'd give anything to stay."

"Cider Cove really is magical." My heart breaks for the poor girl. She was just starting her life here. "I'll tell you what. If you can't find anything at all, I'm sure I can find something for you to do at the inn. That is, if you're interested."

Her face brightens a notch. "Are you kidding? That would be fantastic. I used to work at an inn not that long ago. Oak Falls B&B." She rolls her eyes as she says it as if she'd rather forget the experience, and I totally get that. Working in the hospitality business isn't for everyone. "I'll see what I can drum up, and either way I'll let you know."

"Perfect," I say, just as the man who's spent the last half hour glaring at Lincoln heads over to where the coroner is loading the poor guy onto a gurney.

Julia shakes her head. "And there he goes. I'm telling you, that man wants a front-row seat."

"Who's that?" I ask as I pull Sherlock close by the leash.

"Calvin St. James," she whispers it low. "He was in on some of Lincoln's business dealings. I know for a fact Lincoln invited him out here tonight. I bet Calvin was hoping that he was going to pay him. They went in on the tree lot together, and Lincoln handles the business end of it. I heard them going at it in the house as Lincoln was getting ready."

"The tree lot just above the woods?"

"That's the one. The Sugar Plum Tree Lot. It's their first year, and they've sold more trees since Thanksgiving than they expected. They're having another shipment delivered tomorrow. And that's when a check will need to be written, but Lincoln gave me strict orders not to write it."

"Why would he do that?"

Her shoulders rise to her ears. "Something about payback. I didn't ask many questions when it came to Lincoln and his business relationships. Anyway, I think I'd better get going, too." She nods past the bushes behind me. "I live in the old carriage house in the back. It was a great setup while it lasted."

"Like I said, the inn is open to you. We have cottages we rent out on the grounds, too. We have a lot of long-term rentals."

"Wow, thank you, Bizzy. I guess I won't be losing as much sleep tonight as I thought." We watch as they wheel Lincoln away. ***I'm not sure I would have to begin with.***

Julia takes off into the crowd, and soon they wheel Lincoln right into the back of the coroner's van for one of the last rides of his life.

A flurry of voices goes off in my head all at once as the crowd begins to thicken again. And when it happens this way it's near impossible to tell if it's a man or a woman speaking. Generally I don't know unless I'm standing right in front of them.

Poor Santa keeled over because he ate too many cookies.

Lincoln Brooks is dead because he deserves to be.

Now that was a gift I didn't see coming.

I did it. And I've gotten away with it, too.

I crane my neck into the thicket of people around me, but I can't make out which inner voice belonged to whom.

The kittens in my arms begin to shiver, and Sherlock grows increasingly restless.

It's time to head home and get some rest.

But there's a killer on the loose, and all of Cider Cove will have to sleep with one eye open.

4

The Country Cottage Inn is still in the throes of decking the halls with all the festive glory this season demands and deserves. The inn itself is owned by a wealthy earl from England who has for the most part wisely, or unwisely, left it in my hands. But I don't mind. The Country Cottage Inn is my baby. The building itself is a large stone structure covered with ivy that climbs up to the rooftop, and there are blue cobbled stone paths that lead around the structure. The grounds are located on the white sandy shores of the cove itself, and around most of the periphery of the inn are over three-dozen cottages that are leased out.

"Jordy, don't forget to decorate the upstairs sitting room," I say to the tall man I was married to for all of twenty-four hours. He's boyishly handsome with caramel-colored hair and full cheeks that women crave to pinch. And Jordy is a ladies' man, as in he's been with most of the single women in all of Maine, but that's never stopped a new supply from mobbing him at every turn. Jordy is my best friend Emmie's brother. And years ago the three of us were in Las Vegas where some bad liquor led to some bad decision-making, and before I knew it, an Elvis impersonator pronounced Jordy and me husband and wife. Thankfully, my brother Huxley is a skilled attorney who was quickly able to untangle that unwanted knot. Jordy and I have laughed about it ever since.

Jordy grabs the oversized plastic tub filled with garland and twinkle lights before lifting a brow my way.

"Bizzy? Are you sure we're not overdoing it here?"

"There's no such thing as overdoing it at Christmas. Everyone knows that." I give a quick scratch behind the ears of the two sweet kittens lying on the counter of the reception area. "Besides"—I continue—"the inn is playing host to just about every event under the sun this month. Two of the biggest being the annual cookie exchange and the Let It Snow Ball, the Christmas charity event to help needy families. We're going to have a mass of people coming through those doors and we need to look our Christmas best."

I bend over to kiss one of the kittens on the ear and Fish yowls over at me. Fish has been overseeing their every precious move, but suffice it to say, she isn't nearly as taken with them as I am.

Watch it, Bizzy. Fish licks her paw but doesn't dare take her eyes off of them. ***They bite and claw for no reason. You're liable to lose an eye or a finger. Why don't you take them out back to Critter Corner and forget about them?***

I make a face at my adorably jealous cat. "These little angels would never hurt me." Not intentionally anyhow.

The smaller one lets out a yelp of a meow. ***That's right. Not after that meal you fed us.***

The taller of the two, with the paler face and dark gray mask around her eyes, mewls. ***That's right, Bizzy. We've discussed it and we're not going back to hocking eggnog on the corner. It was too cold for us. There were too many hands tugging and pulling at us. And that woman was mean. Sleeping in the trunk of a car was no picnic.***

I lean in and whisper, "That's never happening again."

The cute little kittens mewl and jump over one another playfully. As soon as I had them in my car last night, I explained that I could hear their thoughts and they've been happily chatting away ever since. They're so adorable, with their fuzzy gray coats and big, wide eyes, I'm half-tempted to keep them both myself. I brought in a tiny cat bed and they've been lounging happily all morning while making the guests smile with their big jade green eyes and the tiny red bows I've attached to each of their collars. I happen to have an entire box of cat supplies for Fish, and I probably have enough collars to strap onto every stray in a ten-mile radius.

"Jordy, can I ask how things are going with Camila?" For the last few weeks they've been seeing one another off and on. I know for a fact Camila isn't all in with Jordy because she's still scheming to sink her claws into Jasper.

Jordy takes a breath as he settles the box of Christmas decorations against the counter for a moment. "She's a tough nut to crack."

"Try harder." I just might gift him a jackhammer as an early Christmas gift to aid in the effort.

"What?" He belts out a quick laugh. "I'm doing my best, Bizzy. Some girls aren't interested in being tied down."

"You weren't interested in being tied down five minutes ago. Maybe you're sending her the wrong signal? When was the last time you went out?"

"I don't know, five, six days ago? We had dinner at the pier."

"Dinner at the pier?" It comes out in a huff, filled with disappointment without meaning to. "Jordy, you have to step up your game. I'm talking romantic things that will knock her socks off like holding hands while ice skating." I think better of it for a second. A dragon like Camila most likely eats hands—she doesn't want to hold them. "Actually, you might want to buy her a very pricy handbag from the mall. A girl like Camila looks as if she's got very expensive taste. I bet the way to her heart is to spend a lot of money."

Jordy grunts as if his wallet were just mortally wounded. Okay, so he doesn't make that much working as a groundskeeper here at the inn, but it's a decent living and he's able to pay all of his bills. Although, if he could pull off a Camila-based miracle, I might just give him a raise.

"Maybe whisk her off to Bear Mountain for a ski trip?" I'm quick to suggest getting her as far away from Cider Cove as possible. "You love to ski. Or take her out with a thermos full of hot cocoa and build snowmen together? In Antarctica."

Someone clears their throat from behind and I turn to find a scorching hot homicide detective looking lean and mean with a crooked smile gliding up his face and my cheeks turn red as a Christmas ornament. Hopefully, he didn't hear the part about Antarctica—or in the least who I'm hoping to send there.

"Giving dating tips, I see." Those crystal gray eyes of his seem to hold a smile all their own before that grin of his melts away. ***I wonder why Bizzy feels the need to give Jordy ideas on where to take Camila? Unless***... He closes his eyes a moment. ***Camila's gotten to Bizzy. I know Camila is still interested in me. But that's not happening. And the last thing I want is for Bizzy to feel insecure.***

An audible groan comes from me. The last thing *I* want is for Jasper to think I'm insecure. Which I'm not. Not all that much anyway. Besides, the wicked witch is all but set to out me and my oddball abilities. I have to be proactive. Antarctica or bust.

"Jordy was asking for suggestions." I shrug over at Jasper while Jordy puts in a mild protest as he heads up the stairs. "I even suggested a *double* date." My entire body heats with the lie. "I mean, it's not like I'm insecure." I offer him a sharp look for even thinking it.

"Double date?" a female voice calls from behind and we turn to find the she-devil herself clad in a red tight-fitted dress. Camila looks as if she just stepped off of a vindictive runway. And by her side is my father's wicked bride-to-be looking every bit as sharp with her dark hair swept up into a chignon, wrapped in a black and white wool houndstooth coat. "Why, I'd love to." Camila doesn't miss a beat. "Jordy and I are free every night this week. We'll leave the ball in your court. Just tell us when and where and we'll be there with sleigh bells on."

Jasper takes a breath. ***Great. I'm positive that neither Bizzy nor I want this. But maybe I'm wrong. Maybe Bizzy does. And who knows? It might be good for Camila to see me with the woman who's stolen my heart.***

I can't help but smile up at him. "We'll get back to you, Camila." Like never. "What can I help you ladies with?" An eviction springs to mind. Although, I suppose since Gwyneth will be my new stepmother, I should have a change of heart with her sooner than later.

Gwyneth peels off her dark leather gloves that adhere to her like a second skin.

She flashes those luminescent eyes my way. "We'll need to see the ballroom. I need to know how many people we can fit in there. I'm still debating on whether or not to have a small, intimate gathering. If we can't squeeze in there, I suppose I can rent out the country club."

A dull laugh rattles in my chest. "Gwyn, the ballroom holds up to four hundred people."

She shrugs over at Camila. "That's far smaller and far more intimate than I imagined, but for the sake of saying we did it, let's head on over."

My mouth falls open. “Grady is in there now helping Nessa with decorations. I’m sure they won’t have any problem with the two of you looking around.”

Both Grady and Nessa help out with the front desk. They’re my right hand when I’m not here. They both graduated from college last year and keep insisting their time at the inn is just a stepping stone, but I don’t know what I would do if they up and left. Fish and Sherlock can only do so much. Although they do make fabulous greeters.

Camila and Gwyneth take off just as Jasper’s phone rings.

He frowns down at the screen. “I’d better take this. I’ll be right back.” He wanders off down the hall just as my sister Macy and my best friend Emmie stroll up with a giant platter of the Country Cottage Café’s latest great treat.

“Gingerbread whoopie pies?” Emmie lands the tray on the counter and I quickly snap up the round treat dusted with powdered sugar. Without hesitating, I shove as much as I can into my mouth and moan my way through it.

Emmie—*Elizabeth*—Crosby and I have been best friends since preschool. We share the same dark, wavy hair and icy blue eyes, and have been mistaken for sisters most of our lives. Since both of our formal first names are Elizabeth, we’ve both stuck to the nicknames our families gifted us.

"Oh, Emmie." I quickly indulge in another bite before continuing. Emmie runs the Country Cottage Café located in the back of the inn. It overlooks the white sandy cove that sits right in front of the expansive Atlantic. And even this time of year it's a treat to sit on the glass-covered porch out back.

Emmie has always had a knack for baking sweet treats, and I've always had a knack for burning them. Not that I've ever let that necrotic little detail detour me from the effort. Emmie and I came up with the idea to make the gingerbread whoopie pies together. And in typical Emmie style, she executed them perfectly.

Macy grunts as she picks up the smaller kitten of the two. "I think what my sister is trying to say is these whoopie pies are to die for. But coming from Bizzy, that's essentially a death threat. I'd get a restraining order if I were you." She gurgles a dark laugh.

Macy is one year older than me, far more hardened by life, and runs off strong coffee and a steady diet of sarcasm. She's dyed her black hair blonde and has spent the last few months entertaining Jamison and Dalton Wilder, two of Jasper's brothers, with her body. It's not a fact I'm proud of. And oddly, she is.

Emmie leans in. "Guess what, Biz? Macy's finally set me up with Jamison."

A shudder runs through me. “Don’t do it. Don’t take any of Macy’s castoffs. They’ve been defiled.” It’s true. But besides that bawdy fact, I don’t want Jamison thinking that Emmie is just as easy as my sister, even if it’s not all that big of a stretch.

Both Emmie and Macy seem to have a propensity to run through men, which I don’t usually mind, but Jasper is involved, thus involving by proxy the delicate state of our rather new relationship.

Emmie makes a face as she picks up the taller kitten. “I like Macy’s castoffs. She warms them up nicely for me. Besides, Jamison and I are going to the Seaview pier. He said there’s a bar with a great happy hour.”

“Happy hour?” I balk. “Come on, Emmie. Make him work a little harder than that.”

“What’s wrong with happy hour?” Emmie brushes a kiss against the tiny kitten’s ear. “Macy says she hits up happy hour on just about every date.”

“First of all, Macy is clinically insane.” I wrinkle my nose over at my sister. “*Sorry*,” I say as I take another quick bite from my gingerbread whoopie pie and Macy waves me off as if it were no big deal. The truth often isn’t. “And second, I don’t want to see my best friend following my sister into a life of depravity. Macy is destined to live the rest of her life alone with a house full of cats.”

"True." Macy snaps up a gingerbread whoopie pie and holds it out to me. "But only because I hate people." She stops shy of taking a bite. "Wait a minute... Aren't you the one who lives alone with a house full of cats? I'll take this one off your hands, by the way." She nuzzles her nose to the tiny cat's snout. "Yes, I will, you little cutie patootie."

"Sorry," I say. "But I can't break up the set."

Emmie squishes the cat she's holding up against her cheek. "What are their names, anyway?"

"They don't have names yet." I reach over to give the one Emmie is holding a quick scratch on the back. "But we should name them quickly. Jasper and I are about to take our entire menagerie to the v-e-t to get f-i-x-e-d."

Macy rolls her eyes. "I'm pretty sure they can't understand you, Bizzy." She looks down at Sherlock Bones. "Hear that, big guy? The next time you walk into this place you'll be a soprano."

Sherlock gives a lazy blink my way. ***Do sopranos get more bacon?***

I nod over to him. "Don't you worry, Sherlock. You'll have all the bacon you want."

Macy and Emmie land the kittens back to their bed and take their platter of gingerbread whoopie pies off to the grand room.

Jasper finishes up with his phone call and heads this way.

"The coroner's report just came in." A comma-like dimple cinches next to his lips. "You were right. Lincoln Brooks was poisoned."

"Knew it," I hiss as I come around the counter and head over to him. "Now what?"

He takes a breath as he glances out the door a moment. "I'd better start questioning the suspects. And there's one that I might need your help with."

"You're letting me help with the case?" A thrill rides through me at the thought.

"No way. There is a very real killer out there, and I want you staying as far away from him or her as possible."

"Well, who's the suspect you want my help with?"

He swallows hard as he looks into my eyes. "It's your mother, Bizzy. It turns out, she's the one that brought over the eggnog from across the street. And right now, she's sitting at the top of the suspect list."

My mother.

At the top of the suspect list.

Just try to keep me out of this investigation, Detective.

I offer him a knowing nod.

It sounds to me, I have a killer to catch.

5

Winter in Cider Cove is as frosty as the arctic, and today is no different. Jasper drove us out to the veterinarian's office this afternoon where both Fish and Sherlock threatened to disown us for allowing those people to cage them up like animals—their words, not mine.

Of course, Jasper and I felt bad, but it's their big day. Jasper and I decided to have both Fish spayed and Sherlock neutered at the very same time. And while we were visiting with the vet, we had the new kittens looked over and vaccinated. And well, they're not all that happy with us either at the moment.

I overheard one of them yearning for better days gone by, sleeping in the trunk of Mary Beth's car. The vet let us know they are British semi-longhaired cats and that they are *purrfectly* healthy—the vet's joke, not mine—but cute nonetheless.

But now that we're through, I convinced Jasper to take us to the Sugar Plum Tree Lot on the edge of town, where rumor has it, the frost is sticking.

"Ooh, it's so beautiful," I sing as we hop out of the car and take in the sheet of white on the ground. It looks magical juxtaposed against the miles and miles of evergreens lining the lot, cut and ready to be delivered to a happy home. There are tons of families here, happily picking out a special tree to call their own. Just beyond the parking lot there are bounce houses for the younger set and a stand that sells both hot cocoa and cookies, which prompts an idea to spring to my mind.

I pull the tiny kittens close to my chest. "Would you look at all of this Christmas magic? I tell you, there is nothing better than the scent of fresh cut pines."

Not true, mewls the smaller one. ***That litter box you set up for us smells like heaven. I want to live there, Bizzy.***

Ooh, me too, the taller one perks up.

"That was lemon-scented kitty litter." I twitch my nose at the two of them. "I'm glad you're easy to please. And I'm really going to have to give you names today."

"Need some help?" Jasper takes the bigger of the two from me. "What kind of names are you thinking?" He gives the red bow on the back of her collar a little tug. "Festive touch, by the way."

"Thanks. And I think their names should be equally festive, like Donner and Vixen, or Noelle and Joy. I don't know... just something along those lines."

"How about Mistletoe and Holly?"

"Hey! I like that. What do you girls think?" I give the shorter one in my arms a quick bounce. "You can be Mistletoe"—I look to her pink-nosed twin—"and you can be Holly."

Mistletoe looks up at me. ***Is that better than Fleabag and Critter?***

A groan comes from me. "Mary Beth was positively monstrous to these poor cuties."

Jasper opens his mouth as if to say something before doing a double take at something over my shoulder. I glance that way to find a man standing by the trailer, talking to a group of women dressed as elves.

It's Calvin St. James, the same man who spent the better part of last night glaring at Lincoln Brooks.

"Bizzy." The tone in Jasper's voice lets me know he's more than suspicious as to why I've dragged him out here. "I recognize that man and I'm guessing you do, too."

"What?" A tiny smile curls on my lips and I can't help but steal a moment to flirt with him. "Fine. I knew he'd be here. But only because last night Lincoln's secretary told me that he and Lincoln own this place together."

A sly smile glides up his cheek. "You spoke to Lincoln's secretary last night?"

"Didn't you?"

His lids hood dangerously low and it sends a spear of heat bisecting across my stomach.

"Okay, I did," he confesses. "I spoke to a few people who happened to be witnesses—in the event you were right and this turned into a homicide investigation." He glances briefly over his shoulder. "But I didn't speak to that guy."

I land my hands over Jasper's chest. "Rest assured, Detective. I didn't ask you here under false pretenses. I really should get a tree for the entry of the inn and a behemoth for the grand room. Do you think it would be too much to get one for the dining room? Oh! And the ballroom. Usually I have Jordy come and pick them up, but I see a bright red sign that says they deliver for free right here in town. It sounds as if I'm in luck."

Jasper's brows depress and he looks dashingly puzzled. Is there a thing this man can't do without looking vexingly sexy?

“So how are we going to do this?” He nods over to the tree lot buzzing with life.

“Oh, I’ll just pick out four or five trees. It shouldn’t take more than a half hour. And by the way, I insist we both get one for ourselves. That way we can order takeout and decorate my tree one night and do the same at your place the next.”

The hint of a lazy grin starts to take over as he leans in. “I meant the investigation, but I like where your head is.” He leans in and steals a quick kiss, and a trio of women glance this way and break out in titters. Believe me when I say Jasper Wilder is more than titter worthy. He pulls back and his eyes gloss over as if he were drugged. “Have I ever mentioned how easily distracted I am whenever you’re around?”

“I do my best to cast a spell.”

“It’s working.” His rough stubble brushes against my cheek. “How do we talk to Calvin? He knows I’m with the Seaview Sheriff’s Department.”

“Oh, right.” I glance over to where he is and find him behind the register at the moment ringing up a customer. “We’ll just tell him the truth. We’re here to pick up a half a dozen trees. And if he’s a true-blue businessman, he’ll love us to death and will tell us anything we want to hear.”

“Let’s do it.”

We start to head over and crest a banner that reads *Welcome to the Sugar Plum Tree Lot, where sugar sweet deals wait for you!* No sooner do we step inside the maze of trees in every shape and size—not to mention the flocked trees of every pastel color—than we see an alarmingly familiar sight.

"Bizzy Baker." Mayor Woods offers a brief smile that stretches across her lips. And behind her pops up her steady Eddie—or steady *Leo* for that matter.

"Mack. Deputy Granger," I all but growl out his name. I'm still not thrilled with him for spilling his darkest secret to that beast he stole from Jasper.

Leo tips his head my way. ***I know you're angry about Camila and her threats, and you have every right to be, but I promise we'll work this out.***

Jasper stiffens by my side. "Mack. Leo." ***There he goes leering at Bizzy again. I am going to have one serious talk with him.*** "Leo"—he ticks his head to the side—"let's talk shop." ***And about the fact you keep ogling my girlfriend like she's a juicy steak set in front of you.***

"Oh—give me Holly," I say, taking the furry beauty from him.

Leo shakes his head as he passes me by. ***Didn't I say he isn't going anywhere?*** He lifts a finger. "I'll be right back."

"So Bizzy"—Mack steps in with her bright red coat, that matching painted on smile—"I suppose you're coming to the annual tree lighting ceremony tomorrow night."

"That I am. And I've got a big sign at the inn inviting all of our guests to join the festivities."

"Good. Emmie said she'd donate four dozen gingerbread whoopie pies to the refreshment table."

"And I approve." Why is she being so amicable?

I squint over at her and a laugh bounces through her.

"Always skeptical of my motives, aren't you, Bizzy?" She gives a little wink. "Fine, I'll come clean." That sickly sweet smile melts right off her face. "Leo's ex keeps fishing around. And I know for a fact she's fishing around your man, too." Her brows peak, giving her that evil villain appeal I'm sure she's after.

"What do you want me to do about it?" I readjust Mistletoe and Holly and dot each of their foreheads with a kiss.

Holly lifts her furry little chin. ***She's wicked, isn't she, Bizzy?***

"On a good day," I whisper into her little ear.

Mack steps in close, like a threat. "What else is there to do but send her packing? Boot her from the inn, Bizzy."

"I can't just boot a guest from the inn."

"Surely you have rules. Invent one and make sure she breaks it before she breaks your heart when she steals Jasper away from you." ***Or worse yet, Leo away from me.***

My lips twitch. "You're really into Leo, aren't you?"

She cranes her neck over my shoulder. "What's there not to like?" She shoots a mean look my way. "And don't get any ideas. Leo is mine," she hisses before strolling off toward the miniature flocked trees.

"Can I help you?" a cheery male voice calls from behind and I turn and jump a little once I see it's Calvin St. James himself. His head is tilted to the side as if he were trying to place me—that or the fact he finds me completely suspicious.

"Oh, right." I give a nervous laugh as I pull Mistletoe and Holly in close. "I manage the Country Cottage Inn." I hold the sweet kittens in my arms and his features soften. "We're here shopping for trees to decorate the inn with."

Calvin St. James looks as if he has ten years on me. He's handsome, dark curly hair, dark button eyes, and thin lips that slide easily in and out of a grin.

"Well, aren't you two the cutest little kittens." He tilts his head as he looks to me once again. "Wait a minute. You were there last night, weren't you?" There's a slight look of relief on his face as if the last piece of the puzzle fits. Little does he know the puzzle I'm working on—the one in which I help remove my mother from the suspect list—is still taking shape. I'd say Calvin is most likely an important piece himself.

"Candy Cane Lane?" I give a few innocent blinks. "It seems the entire town was there. Oh! The cats. Yes, one of the neighbors gave them to me. There was a horrible accident there last night."

He nods as his features darken. "Lincoln Brooks. He was my business partner." ***A louse and a cheat, but I'll leave that out for now.*** "Did you know him?"

"No, not really. Oddly enough, my mother dated him once upon a time." Regretfully. I believe she used the words *louse* and *cheat* to describe him a time or two herself.

A small laugh bounces from him. "Don't worry. He dated just about everybody's mother." ***That's why he was such a lousy businessman. He was far too busy taking care of his physical needs to pay attention to the bottom line. And now I get to suffer for it. But not for long. Life is sweeter just***

one day after his passing. And in just a few weeks, it will be sweeter still.

I clear my throat. "It sounds like Lincoln really got around. I met his girlfriend last night. Trixie, I think she said her name was."

He closes his eyes a moment. "Trixie Jolly-Golightly?" He twitches his brows suggestively. "That's her dancer name."

Figures. My mother is always right.

"Oh?" I try to sound surprised. "Well, that's how she introduced herself. Do you know her real name?"

"Nope. Doubt Lincoln did either. But I think we both know he wasn't all that interested in hearing the truth from her." ***Or anybody else for that matter.***

"What does that mean?" I lean in, anxious to hear anything he has to tell me.

"It means I think she was on his payroll." He nods heavily as if I should know what that means. "She's a pretty girl."

"Yes, well, he had money. Sometimes pretty girls like Trixie are attracted to that." I bite down on my lip. "Any news on how he died?"

He blinks back. ***Is she kidding? I thought it was evident. And if it wasn't, then it will be once they do the autopsy.***

My lips part, unsure of which direction to go in. "I mean, I thought he had a heart attack, but rumors are swirling he was murdered." I shrug it off. "Cider Cove is a small, small town."

He averts his eyes. "Don't I know it. I live out in Whaler's Cove. Cider Cove is—*was* Lincoln's stomping ground. He's the one that owns the land we're standing on. I'm the one he utilized to do all the grunt work."

"What happens to you now that he's gone? Are you out of a job?"

"Nope. We owned a fifty-fifty split on most things we were involved with. I spoke to my lawyer and he said I should be able to file for full ownership unless someone contests it."

He spoke with his lawyer? Lincoln hasn't been dead for twenty-four hours. It's not even one in the afternoon.

Mistletoe burrows her head against my neck. ***I think he sounds guilty, Bizzy. Get Jasper to cuff him so we can get back to the cottage and enjoy some more of that Fancy Beast cat food.***

It sounds as if they're taking a page right out of Sherlock's bacon-laced playbook.

"Good luck to you," I say to Calvin. "I hope you don't miss out on a single property that's due to you."

Oh, I won't, sweetie. His lips curl at the thought. ***I've all but ensured it.***

He nods my way. "I'm sure it will work out exactly how it's intended. Go ahead and pick out as many trees as you like. They're on me."

"Oh no, I insist on paying."

He shrugs as he squints into the crowd. "Have it your way. But I'll take the biggest one off the tab. You can't stop me." He gives a little wink. "And you'll be seeing me again. I've already bought a ticket to the charity function at the Country Cottage Inn. I guess you could say we'll be spending Christmas Eve *Eve* together."

"And we're going to have lots of fun," I tease. "Bring a fat wallet. All proceeds go to needy families in the area."

"I sure will!"

He starts to take off, and I block his path.

"Hey, Calvin? If Lincoln was murdered, who do you think did it?"

"You know"—he blows out a quick breath as he looks to some invisible horizon—"I'd bet it was those nutty neighbors. They were feuding pretty bad. If I had a dime for every time Lincoln complained about his ex and her new husband, I might really be a rich man by now." ***And I will be soon enough.*** He offers me a brief salute. "Take your time." He jogs off to the register where a bevy of customers have lined up.

Jasper comes back and groans as he watches Calvin take off.

He frowns over at him. "I missed it, didn't I?"

"Don't worry. Something tells me you'll be talking to Calvin a lot."

Calvin St. James is hiding something sinister—something to do with money. And money is always a great motivator for murder.

I'll let Jasper winnow out the details on that one. For now, it looks as if we'll need to make another trip down Candy Cane Lane to speak with the Bronsons.

They are, in fact, looking guilty as sin.

6

The weather outside has taken a turn for the dark and sinister, much like the emotional climate in Cider Cove. Christmas feels as if it's sneaking up on me far faster than ever should be allowed. There are still presents to be bought and wrapped—not to mention Cider Cove's annual cookie exchange will be taking place in just a few days, right here at the inn.

As soon as I got back from the tree lot, I took Mistletoe and Holly to my cottage where they've been happily napping ever since. But at the moment I'm standing in the brightly lit interior of the Country Cottage Café, helping with the afternoon rush as Emmie and I ring up a small crowd of guests. The café is brightly lit and the scent of those gingerbread whoopie pies infiltrates through the air, enlivening the senses. There's a large chalkboard that stands on an easel and highlights all of the holiday-themed specials for the month, and almost all of the bistro tables strewn about are filled to capacity with happy customers noshing away on their meals.

No sooner does the activity at the register die down than Georgie waltzes into the establishment in a bright green kaftan and a string of gold garland around her neck.

"Yuletide greetings!" She wags a piece of mistletoe over her head and blows both Emmie and me a kiss.

Emmie giggles at the sight. "Let me guess. You're tracking down all the handsome men in Cider Cove and threatening them with a little holiday delight?"

"You bet your blue-eyed tooshie, missy." Georgie gives a sly wink. "Now where are those cute kitties of yours, Bizzy? Everyone knows kittens are a man magnet. I'll have an entire line of men trying to break down my door by midnight once I work my trifecta of holiday magic—with this outfit, this seasonal sprig, and those cagey cats, I'll be fighting off a proposal by the new year."

Emmie and I share a warm laugh.

"The kittens are napping at my place. But can I get you anything from the café while you're here? The usual?"

"Nah, I've gotta run. I still have a few hours of work to put in today. By this weekend the first segment of the mural will be completed."

Georgie has been working for months on a city-funded beautification effort along one of the tall retaining walls right here on Main Street. She's creating a glass mosaic that will span an entire city block, featuring oceanic scenes that are sure to attract tourists to the area.

Emmie leans in. "An entire segment? Congratulations. How many segments are there?"

"Fifty-two." Georgie doesn't miss a beat.

"Geez." I grimace. "Georgie, this is going to take you a couple of years or longer to finish. They're not paying you hourly, are they?"

She belts out a maniacal laugh and shoots me with her fingers. "Now you're picking up what I'm laying down." She looks to Emmie. "One hot java and two of those gingerbread whoopie miracles to go, please. I can't stand around here all day doing nothing. I've got to go *there* and stand around all day doing nothing."

Emmie tips her head. "I'll get right on it."

She takes off and I lean in. "So, are you ready for the big day? Have you gotten any Christmas shopping done?"

"Yes and no. Yes, I'm ready for the big day—because who isn't ready for Christmas? And no, I haven't even started my shopping yet. I'll admit, I'm no good at figuring out what people want."

"Sure, you are. I love the wish jar you gave me last year."

It's true. Georgie gifted me a Mason jar with miniature twinkle lights inside and instructed me to speak a wish into it every night. It's an adorable concept and the jar is beautiful. And when I look at Jasper, I know in my heart every last wish was granted.

She shrugs. "I gave everyone a wish jar last year. It was one of my best gifts and no one lost a finger."

"Georgie, I'm sure you always give good gifts—and no one loses a finger over it."

"Not true," she says just as Emmie slides a coffee and two gingerbread whoopie pies her way. "One year I gave everyone a paring knife as sharp as a razor. My aunt Hilda sliced off a finger before she finished unwrapping it. The knife was so sharp she didn't even notice the finger was gone until she was covered with blood."

Both Emmie and I groan in unison.

Before I can say a word about Georgie's questionable gift-giving choices, Mom dashes into the café, rushing over in a panic.

"Bizzy! Oh, thank goodness you're here." Her hair is blown sideways and her coat is crooked as if she ran all the way over. "I just spoke with that boyfriend of yours. Can you believe they have reason to suspect me of tampering with the eggnog?" she hisses the words out so fast it sounds like one long sentence.

I make my way around the counter and pull her in.

"I'm so sorry. He mentioned something this morning, but I didn't think he was serious. Mom, I know you had nothing to do with Lincoln Brooks' death." I nod over at her as if demanding that she reassures me of this.

Instead, she shudders and glances away.

Sure, I wanted to kill him. I might have even rooted for someone else to do it.

"Ree Baker!" Georgie practically dances a jig she's so excited. "Have you been accused of a homicide? Oh, this month is off to a murderously delicious start." She pulls her along by the hand. "Let's take a seat and you can tell me all about it. I'll share my magical whoopie pies with you and you can tell me how you kicked his old keister to the other side."

Leo Granger strides into the café and I shoot him a disparaging look.

"Go ahead, Mom. I'll be right there," I tell her. "Emmie"—I lean toward my bestie—"would you bring my mother a candy cane latte? I've got a bone to pick with someone."

Leo heads this way with a smirk and I can't help but smirk right back.

"Well, if it isn't Granger the supernatural ranger," I say. "I hope you're ready to speak up, because you owe me answers."

His cheek flickers. "You'll get more mileage out of me with donuts."

"I'll do you one better. Gingerbread whoopie pies. It's the best thing going just this side of heaven." I pop three on a tray and slide them his way.

"I think I'll need some coffee to wash this down. This looks amazing, Bizzy."

"Good," I say as I quickly pour him a cup of candy cane hot java cheer. "Because I have a feeling you'll be filling my ears with a few amazing tidbits you failed to mention."

I waste no time shuttling him to a table near the window, far enough from my mother and Georgie and the unintentional homicide they're trying to dissect.

I lean in. "As if getting my mother off of Jasper's suspect list wasn't enough, I've got Camila Ryder and her very real threats to contend with. Why in the world would you tell her about your ability to read minds? Are you nuts? You should always deny, deny, *deny*. I didn't need some supernatural rulebook to tell me that one. It's what's kept me from being the starring act in some government circus sideshow."

He all but rolls his eyes before indulging in a hearty bite of the gingerbread wonder before him.

"Oh, man." A deep moan evicts from him. "You weren't kidding. This is the best thing going just this side of heaven."

"I'm glad you think so," I say, pulling his tray over to myself and dangling those luscious sweet treats just out of reach. "Because if you want the rest of them, you'll answer my question."

He glowers at me a moment. "Fine. I didn't tell her." He winces. "Not directly. I was having some fun with her, playing a few games."

"Leo," I groan. "So you were coming across as the man who magically knew what she was thinking? And you took it too far." I shake my head over at him. "But why admit it when she caught on? Once you cross that line, there's no going back. Like with Georgie and me. And look where that landed me. Having a conversation with you while my boyfriend's wicked ex threatens to out me."

He gives a little shrug. "I'm sorry, Bizzy. You're right. In hindsight, I should have denied it, laughed it off. But my ego was swelling. And at the time, she was still up for stroking it."

A flurry of words gets trapped in my throat and I gag on them.

"Listen"—I lean in hard—"I'm not even a little interested in hearing about what that woman was stroking. How do I get her off my back?"

"You said it yourself. Deny, deny, deny." He shrugs.

"You're so right." I sag at the thought of having no other option. "Honestly, how did that woman turn into my worst nightmare?"

His brow rises as he glances to the entry. "Don't look now, but your worst nightmare just walked in." He closes his eyes a moment. "Also, we can't meet like this anymore. Jasper threatened my position at the department."

"What?" I squawk myself right out of my seat. "Leo, he would never have you fired. He's not like that."

His dark eyes meet with mine. "He's very much like that. And he has the power to do it, too." He takes a deep breath. "Look, we can have clandestine conversations in passing, mind to mind. But I'm afraid this will have to be our last rodeo sharing coffee and the world's best gingerbread whoopie pies." He pulls the tray over to him once again just as a shadow darkens our little corner of the café.

How do you like that? Camila practically hums with glee internally. ***I've got her so hopped up on fear she can't stand to be near my shadow.***

Isn't that the truth.

"And on that note." I don't even bother acknowledging Camila as I brush past her and land all the way across the dining room seated right before my rather panicked mother and Georgie.

"Bizzy"—Mom practically hisses my name—"do something. I can't be named a suspect in a homicide investigation. Cider Cove is a small town. It will ruin my reputation and your sister's—and *yours* by proxy. Believe me when I say Lather and Light will suffer."

I cringe at the thought. Lather and Light is Macy's soap and candle shop located just up the way.

"Mom, why are you a suspect? And how were you handing out the eggnog? You were with me when we saw both Lincoln and Dexter drinking it."

She glances to the ceiling.

If I knew what would have become of that man, I would have watched the show from across the street.

And that right there assures me my mother had nothing to do with this—I think.

Georgie bumps her arm to mine. "Your mother admitted to hauling over a pitcher of eggnog. That's how she got him." She winks over at the woman the Seaview County Sheriff's Department is so quick to finger for the debacle. "Now tell us how you did it. Wolfsbane? Arsenic? Good old-fashioned household bleach?"

Mom's mouth rounds out in horror. "Would you hush? There are other people around in the event you were too out of your cracked skull to notice. And for your information, I didn't do anything. I met up with Mary Beth across the street at the snack stand, and she asked if I could lend her a hand. She mentioned Dexter and Lincoln were going at it, and I suggested we take some eggnog over and cool them off."

"So it was your idea." I bite down over my lip. "Do you think maybe she coaxed you into it? Like maybe she pointed to the eggnog?"

She makes a face as she struggles to recall. "You know, come to think of it, she suggested the hot cocoa. It was me who thought the eggnog would cool them off."

"So she did suggest a drink." I shake my head. "If Mary Beth knew she was going to poison Lincoln, maybe she was trying to set you up? Mom, did you and Mary Beth have any problems?"

Georgie slaps the table. "Ree, you slept with her husband! Of course, she hated you and wanted to peg you for his murder. It's a classic tale of love gone awry. Face it, Ree, you're the other woman. The universe will side with the wife on this one."

Mom's eyes enlarge the size of one of those whoopie pies. "The universe will side with me once I decide to poison you. How about coming to my place later for eggnog? I've got a jug of bleach just waiting to right all the wrongs in this world."

Georgie all but purrs at the offer, her eyes squinted with mischievous delight. "I say bring on the eggnog, but just know that anything with a high dairy content makes me lose my good senses, and word to the murderous wise, I travel with a butcher knife in my tote bag."

Mom groans, "Bizzy, please tell Jasper this whole thing is ridiculous. It's obvious Mary Beth had it in for the guy. I bet she and Dexter staged that whole argument right before baiting me over to that silly stand of hers."

I suck in a quick breath. "How did she bait you?"

Georgie snorts. "I bet she waved a bottle of your mother's favorite vodka and she came running like a deer after a headlight."

Mom nearly tips over, she's so incensed. "Georgie, I don't drink vodka. Nor do I imbibe in anything remotely fermented."

"Really?" Georgie tips her head suspiciously. "Then how, pray tell, do you keep up with that young stud of yours from the hours of twelve to six a.m.?"

I cover my ears a moment. The last thing I want to know is details on how my mother keeps up with my boyfriend's *brother* during those unholy hours.

"Never mind that," I say. "Mom, how did Mary Beth bait you?"

Her mouth opens and closes. "Okay, fine. She didn't bait me. I parked across the street from the stand and was about to buy myself a nice cup of hot cocoa when she asked for help. And I simply picked up a pitcher and followed her to Lincoln's house. I set the pitcher down on a table near Lincoln's porch, and that's when I saw Lincoln and Dexter going at it. I thought I might be the one to put a stop to it, so I went over."

"And that's when I saw you."

Georgie wraps an arm around me. "So what's our next move, Detective Baker?"

My phone buzzes, and it's a text from the vet letting me know it's time to pick up Fish and Sherlock.

"I have to run," I say as I give my mother's hand a quick squeeze from across the table. "Don't worry about a thing. I'll clear things up with Jasper."

Georgie gives a husky laugh that qualifies as an innuendo all on its own.

She gives a sly smile my way. "It must be nice to have boyfriends with homicidal fringe benefits. Hear that, Ree? You have a get-out-of-murder-charges-free card because Bizzy is getting *busy* with the po-po."

Mom growls as if there just might be another homicide afoot.

"I'll see you both soon." I pop up out of my seat. "Try not to rack up a body count while I'm gone."

I have a feeling exactly who I need to speak with to get my mother out of this murderous mess, and it's not Jasper.

Mary Beth Bronson, I'm coming for you.

But first, I need to come up with an extra helping of Fancy Beast cat food and a truckload of bacon as I cuddle with two sweet beasts that need all of my love and affection right now.

And the best part of all—Jasper will be right there with me.

7

Fish yowls up at me as I hold her like a baby wrapped in her favorite blanket.

I may never forgive you.

Sherlock lets out a meager bark from across the room.

I may never forgive you.

I groan as I snuggle against Jasper. "They may never forgive us."

He chuckles at the thought. "They'll forgive us." He reaches over and gives Sherlock a pat. There's a large plastic cone around his neck, preventing him from licking himself into regret and damnation—those were the vets exact words, not mine.

"Maybe—in a decade," I say, carefully placing Fish onto the sofa next to me. The vet did caution me against holding her too much and said she would do best placed in her bed. Little does the vet know the only bed that Fish has claimed ownership of is *my* bed. And if I'm not in it, she's convinced the entire contraption doesn't function properly. Besides, her official bed, the tiny padded ball of fluff I purchased for her a few months back, is currently occupied with a pair of sleeping kittens that have stolen my heart.

Jasper and I had Chinese food delivered straight to my cottage from the Dragon Express, and we indulged until each delicious box of Eastern Hemisphere-inspired joy was devoured. My quaint little cottage is decorated in a shabby chic style with its frilly curtains and yellow and white plaid sofa. But this time of year I've pulled out every Christmas tchotchke known to man. I've decorated the mantel with garland and lights, and there's a giant snow globe on the coffee table that encapsulates a town that reminds me of Cider Cove in the winter.

Jasper pulls me in close and his lids drop down a notch, hooding over those glowing eyes that search my features as if he were trying to memorize them.

"Has anyone told you you're beautiful today?" His cheek glides up one side and I can see the naughty intent in his eyes. I'm really liking the naughty intent.

"Not since you mentioned it yesterday," I whisper.

"You're beautiful, Bizzy." He lands a heated kiss to my lips. "I'll make sure you hear it every day."

I clear my throat. "So what was it that you and Leo were discussing at the tree lot this morning?" This might be a perfect time to reassure him he has nothing to worry about, thus securing Leo's position at the sheriff's department.

Jasper pulls back to get a better look at me. ***Why would she ask about that?***

He presses out a quick breath. "Just some department business." His lips twist. ***I'm not about to tell her that I threatened him within an inch of his career if he so much as looks in her direction. He's diabolical. I wouldn't put it past him to tell her just about anything to wedge his way into her life. The guy is a plague between us and he needs to be stopped. And—I stopped him, all right. One more wayward glance and he's on the next train back to Sheffield. We don't need him in Seaview anyway.***

"Department business." I shudder as I repeat the words. "For a second, I thought you were threatening the poor guy with his job just because he bothered to look in my direction." I give a quick wink and Jasper's eyes widen the size of fried egg dumplings.

"You know, Bizzy, it's like you can read my mind."

I'm about to laugh off the idea when that conversation I had with Leo comes back to me. This is exactly how he said it started with him and Camila. Dear Lord, I'm headed down the same dark path I berated him over. This is not going to end well unless I nip it in the bud right now.

"I'm just a good guesser." A good guesser? Kill me. I scoot back a notch so I can get a better look at him. "Jasper, I need my mother wiped off that suspect list. It's Christmas. She should be stressing out about the gifts my sister will undoubtedly reject rather than whether or not she can barter cigarettes in the prison commissary."

"The answer would be a hard no to that last one." He glances to the floor a moment. "As far as taking her off the suspect list, I'm sorry, Bizzy, but she was there. She admitted to bringing the eggnog across the street, and she has a romantic history with the deceased. She checks off a lot of boxes."

"Did the coroner's report say what Lincoln was poisoned with?"

He gives a solemn nod, his fingers absentmindedly spinning slow concentric circles against the back of my neck. "Methanol poisoning—antifreeze. Along with another compound, a toxin we're still looking into. Something that expedited the process, no doubt."

"Antifreeze?" Ironically, my muscles freeze at the mention of it. "No wonder poor Lincoln could hardly choke the stuff down."

"I don't know about that. Most methanol is odorless and doesn't leave much of a flavor. He genuinely may not have appreciated Mary Beth's eggnog."

"Mary Beth," I practically hiss her name out. "Jasper, she coerced my mother into bringing the eggnog across the street, and we both know Mary Beth definitely had a romantic history with the deceased. They were married."

"I know." He shakes his head as his chest expands with his next deep breath. "I mean, the fact she lives with her current husband in the same house that she was married to Lincoln in—well, it might have bothered most men. I can see where the contention lay between them. And, add in Dexter and you have a perfect storm. It was no wonder they were battling it out on the lawn that night. I'm surprised it wasn't a daily occurrence."

"But why would Mary Beth want him dead? I mean, he's not her husband anymore. He hasn't been for years. You would think Dexter would be used to him by now, too. And that whole house-decorating thing? They're not novices at that either. They've been doing it for over a decade. Why now?"

"I don't know. They don't have children. They no longer share property. Both the Bronsons and Lincoln are doing well for themselves financially. It's a real head scratcher." He steals another kiss and this time he lingers.

Sherlock moans, ***I want to scratch my head, Bizzy. Take this wall of torment away from me. I'll share my bacon with you. Heck, I'll give all of my bacon to Fish if it helps remove this contraption. Georgie calls it the cone of shame, Bizzy! I can't be seen in public like this.***

A tiny laugh rumbles through me.

Jasper pulls me onto his lap. "What's so funny?"

"You," I say, giving his tie a quick tug. "Now, tell me again, Detective. What do I have to do to get my mother off the suspect list?"

A lazy grin glides over his face as he touches a finger to his lips. "You can start here. But it's going to take a lot of convincing."

A dark laugh rumbles from me. "Good thing I've got all night."

Sometimes you need to do what you need to do to protect your mother.

And ironically, I won't be thinking about her one bit as I do it.

8

If there is one thing I look forward to each and every year, it's the annual tree lighting ceremony right here in Cider Cove. For some reason, it's always felt like a unifying event. No matter how busy we are with life, it seems the entire town comes out to witness the official kickoff to a brand new Christmas season. It also signifies the three-week period where townies and tourists alike can enjoy horse-drawn carriage rides up and down Main Street. The carriages are something straight out of a fairytale with twinkle lights woven through the spokes of the enormous wheels, as well as the canopy that covers the majestic carriage. The horses are dusted with iridescent glitter and shine under the streetlights with all the appeal of a mythological creature. I think I can say with all honesty there is no place like Cider Cove at Christmastime.

Jasper had to work late but assured me he'd be at the park in plenty of time to see the seventy-foot evergreen illuminated in all its holiday glory.

Georgie and Emmie help me bring platters of the Country Cottage Café's gingerbread whoopie pies over to the refreshment table. Emmie and I thought we'd spread a little good cheer and make double the amount of whoopie pies than we originally intended to bring. Hopefully, people will find them so irresistible they'll storm the café to pick up a dozen or so for their holiday parties. Even though the Country Cottage Café is attached to the inn, it's open to the general public and we always appreciate their business.

Georgie elbows me in the ribs as soon as we put the whoopie pies down.

"So what's gonna happen?" she whispers through the side of her mouth like a bad ventriloquist as we take in the ever-growing crowd.

The tree lighting ceremony itself is taking place at the city park that stands at the edge of Main Street, and all of the streetlights are decorated with a giant wreath. A chain of twinkle lights entwined with garland is strung all the way up and down the street in every direction you look. And yet, the most stunning sight to see is that horse-drawn carriage as it clip-clops its way over, lighting up the entire vicinity with a soft incandescent glow.

Emmie leans over to Georgie. "I'll tell you what's going to happen. You're going to help me man the refreshment table in the event that killer wants to come back and do us all in."

Georgie gags at the thought. "I don't know why I didn't think of that. It's a brilliant idea. If the killer were smart, they would think so, too," she says, tapping the side of her head. "A mass homicide will throw the sheriff's department for a loop."

"Oh, Georgie," I groan. "Let's pray this killer isn't half as bright."

I spot a familiar looking woman with short dark hair who looks as if she's bossing an entire crowd of people around. I don't know Mary Beth all that well, but every time I see her it looks as if she's herding a crowd. I take it she likes to be in charge. I'm betting she likes things to go her way, perhaps even things of a nefarious nature, like planting my mother at the nexus of a murder scene, or ending Lincoln's life because she felt it was time for him to go. That is, of course, if she did it. And I know for a fact my mother *didn't*, so that about narrows the field.

I snatch a few gingerbread whoopie pies off a platter and land them on a dessert plate.

"I'll be right back, ladies," I say, not taking my eyes off Mary Beth.

Emmie follows my gaze and growls, "Take your time, Bizzy. Justice can't be rushed." She sucks in a quick breath. "Oh, I almost forgot to tell you. Jamison will be here tonight. It's our first official quasi-date. Do I look okay?" She cranes her neck and looks into my eyes as if she were looking into a mirror.

"Go easy on him, Em. I'm serious about Jasper. It's bad enough Macy ate her way through his brothers like a bag of salty potato chips. Not to mention the carnage my mother is causing with Max."

Emmie winces. "Do you think that's going to last?"

I blow out a breath as I contemplate it. "With Ree Baker, you never know. If she's consistently anything, she's consistently unpredictable."

Georgie snatches up a whoopie pie herself. "Oh, it's going to last. Ree just started a whole new cardio routine to keep up with the demands that boy places on her body."

"And on that note"—I take a step in the opposite direction—"wish me luck. I'd rather hang out with a killer than discuss my mother's reasons for an increase in her cardio."

Emmie belts out a laugh. “It sounds like you need some cardio yourself!” she calls out as I disappear into the crowd.

The icy air whips around me, burning my lungs, assuring me that the walk across the street will be cardio enough on a frozen night like this.

Mary Beth stands with a group of women about the same age as they carry on a conversation in front of the darkened tree that’s about to ignite the night with the power of a thousand candles. I’ve seen this group of mothers around town together. They all have kids about the same age at the same schools.

Just as I open my mouth to call out to Mary Beth, an all too familiar body gets in my way and I groan at the sight of her.

“Camila,” I say, struggling to look past her in the event Mary Beth decides to bolt like the fugitive she is.

Camila glides to the right and effectively blocks my line of vision. She’s wrapped in an emerald green coat, and her hair is wild and wavy as it hovers above her like tentacles as if it had a life of its own.

“Well, if it isn’t Bizzy Baker.” She purses her bright red lips. ***I’m sure you’re just thrilled to bump into me, aren’t you, Dizzy?***

I'm tempted to say something, but those words I uttered to Leo come back to me. *Deny, deny, deny.*

"I don't know why you're staring at me that way." I cinch a smile. "If you're looking for Jasper, he's not here. Now, if you'll excuse me—"

She steps in close and snatches me by the arm, nearly sending my whoopie pies to the ground.

"No, I will not excuse you, Bizzy." Her smile tightens. "You and I both know your little anomaly won't be a secret for long. Have you thought about what I said?"

"I'm not afraid of you or your threats, Camila. I'm not leaving Jasper just because you discovered that you made a grave mistake in your relationship. And besides that, Jasper is a grown man. If he wanted to be with you, he would. Nobody is holding a gun to his head. He's with me because he wants to be. I'm sorry if that hurts you, but it's a fact. I can't change it, and neither can you. No amount of threats or whatever other emotional toxins you have brewing will make him love you." I try to step around her and she steps in close.

"You're right. I can't make him love me, Bizzy. But I don't have to. He never stopped. What we have is real. It's deep." ***You're going to leave him, Bizzy. And if you don't, I will ruin anything you and Jasper think is***

true. Consider this a fair warning. And if you don't comply, I'll be forced to end things for you.

"You wish you had that much power," I say without thinking, and my lips curl at the edges as I take in the desperation she's exuding.

"Knew it!" The whites of her eyes flash wildly.

I blink back with feigned surprise. "I don't know what you're talking about." My shoulder clips hers as I make my way across the street and into the mommy hive as I come up on my intended target.

"Mary Beth." I try to sound cheery as the stony-faced brunette snaps to attention. "So glad you came out tonight. Care to try a gingerbread whoopie pie? They were made fresh this afternoon at the Country Cottage Café."

"Oh, Bizzy." A warbling moan evicts from her throat. "You know my weakness. I'm all about the sweets. Sweet like me." She gives a quick wink as she snaps one up and takes a bite. "Wow," she howls through a mouthful. "That is insane! I'd kill for that recipe."

An activity I'm wondering if she's far too familiar with.

I make a face without meaning to. "You're in luck. We're giving a copy to everyone who attends the Let It Snow Ball." Or at least we are now. "All ticket sales and proceeds from the silent auction go straight to benefit needy families in the community. You won't want to miss it. It's for a great cause."

"My husband and I will both be there. We've already purchased tickets. Unfortunately, gone are the days I could drag my kids off to events like that. They're teenagers now. Two boys and a girl. They care more about parties and friends than they do hanging out with their parents at a charity event. How about you? Any kids?"

"Nope. Just cats. Two of which are the angels you gave me. They're doing great, by the way. They're home tonight with my cat, Fish, and my boyfriend's dog, Sherlock. Fish and Sherlock just got fixed, and those sweet kittens are doing their best to cheer them up." It's true. Mistletoe and Holly are large and in charge, and about as maternal as can be. Fish finds it mildly annoying, and Sherlock isn't impressed with their lack of ability to bring him bacon.

Mary Beth scoffs. "I really don't care how they're doing. My eyes water just thinking about them." She takes another bite out of her whoopie pie.

"I'm sorry about your ex-husband." I give a little shrug, and her eyes harden over mine for a moment.

"Lincoln?" Her upper lip tugs to the side as if the thought of him sickened her. "I'm sorry, too." ***Sorry this is starting to drag out. And a homicide investigation? It's the last thing I would have***

thought. Lord knows we worked him up enough for anyone who was there to think he had a proper heart attack. What is it with the Seaview Homicide Division? Don't they have better things to do than stir up drama during the holidays? "He had it coming, though." Her eyes widen a notch, and I can't help but wonder if she meant to let it slip out.

"What makes you say that?" She did say it out loud. It's fair game of me to ask.

"It's no secret he had enemies." Her lips crimp as she inspects the bustling crowd.

A group of carolers stride by, singing a chipper version of "God Rest Ye Merry Gentlemen," and I step in closer to Mary Beth as to not miss a single word.

"What enemies?"

She squints into the crowd as if she were looking at one of them right now, and I follow her gaze directly to the woman who bore me.

"Oh, she didn't do it."

Mary Beth averts her eyes. "That's funny, I didn't accuse her. But, well, she was there." ***The little tramp couldn't wait to get her claws into Lincoln once the ink was dry on our divorce papers. She deserves everything she has coming.***

"That's my mother," I say as her mind blinks to a wash of white noise—a telltale sign that I've thrown her for a loop. "And I'm positive she didn't kill anyone. Did you see anything funny going on that night? Word on the street is he was poisoned."

"Your mother, huh?" ***I should have guessed. The annoying fruit doesn't fall far from the annoying tree.*** She takes a breath. "I hate to break it to you, Bizzy, but it was your mother who hauled the eggnog from across the street."

"Who poured it?"

She swallows hard. ***I'm not admitting anything.***

She shrugs. "There was a crowd around the porch. It could have been anyone. Trixie, that trashy vixen Lincoln insisted on spending all his time with, was there. She had full access to his credit cards. I heard them arguing just as Dexter and I arrived across the street—something about him cutting her off. It sounds as if that free ride on Lincoln's American Express Black Card had come to an abrupt end. You get used to a certain lifestyle, and well, it can be hard returning to nothing. I wouldn't be surprised if she was angry enough to spike his drink with venom. And what did he think would happen hanging around a woman like that? There's only one thing she was after, and it wasn't what Lincoln had hiding under that Santa suit. She was out for his money if you ask me. Lincoln cut her off, and then she cut him off—from the planet."

The crowd around us begins to cheer as Mayor Woods takes up the microphone and welcomes everyone to the event. She starts in on a countdown from ten as a mass of bodies push between Mary Beth and me, taking her away in the swell.

I turn around and my eyes hook onto a tall, dark, and startlingly handsome homicide detective as he strides this way. Jasper looks dressed to kill with his long dark coat thrown over his midnight-colored suit. His dark hair reflects the moonlight, and his eyes shine like stars, giving him that cutthroat sexy appeal. Half the women here are turning their heads in his direction despite the fact the tree in question we're all here to ogle is clearly in the opposite direction.

"Detective Wilder," I say as I meet him halfway and he wraps his strong arms around me.

"Bizzy Baker." His lids hood low and he gives me a little spin as the crowd hits the end of their countdown and the world around us lights up like noonday.

The tall noble demands our attention with white lights dotting it like stars in a tree-shaped galaxy.

The carolers ignite the air with a cheery rendition of "Deck the Halls," and the crowd begins to sing along.

"You made it." I throw my arms around his neck.

"I wouldn't miss it."

"So what do you think?" I bite down on my lip playfully.

"I don't think I've ever seen anything more beautiful," he says, examining my features.

"Jasper, you're not looking at the tree."

He gives a sly grin. "Is there a tree?"

A shadow dampens the light from the holiday spectacle, and we look over to find Camila holding hands with Jordy.

Poor guy looks like a little boy being dragged around by his angry older sister.

"Jasper"—she bears her fangs at him—"Bizzy and I were just shoring up details for our double date tomorrow night." She looks my way. "Dinner at The Station at seven works great for both Jordy and me. Thank you again for inviting us."

I can't help but scoff at that one.

Behave, Bizzy. Camila bears those dark eyes into mine. ***This was your idea and you like it.***

Jordy nods our way. "Yes, thank you, Bizzy. I've been meaning to check that place out." He glances to Jasper. ***Plus, this way I can finally vet this guy.***

Camila gives a wave with her fingers. "See you both tomorrow night. We're looking forward to it."

We watch as they dissolve into the crowd and Jasper takes a breath.

"Do I want to know what that was about?" ***And here I thought the worst thing that was going to happen this month was my mother getting hitched to someone she hardly knows—Bizzy's womanizing father of all people.***

I give a little shrug. "And here I thought the worst thing that was going to happen this month was your mother and my father making it official."

He bucks with a silent laugh. "We really are on the same wavelength. You sure about tomorrow night with those two? My ex and yours? It sounds like double trouble."

"Oh, it will be." I catch a glimpse of Mack and Leo standing by the tree as they entertain a small crowd, and a thought comes to me. "But, I'm sure about it." I think it's time to employ Mack and that special brand of fury only she can provide. Mack wants to get rid of Camila just as much as I do. I say the sooner, the better.

A flurry of internal voices erupts around me as I struggle to make out where they're coming from.

There she is.

Boy, wouldn't I love to take a bite out of that detective. Arrest me, please.

Nobody seems to care about the egregious electrical waste that this holiday season seems to sponsor.

Bizzy is nosying around, scratching away at something that doesn't concern her.

I'll have to keep an eye out on that girl.

Or perhaps, I'll have to kill her, too.

I snap my head in every direction at once to see who could be looking my way, but the crowd is far too thick to make out a single thing.

Someone killed Lincoln Brooks.

And now they're gunning for me.

9

No, no, Fish growls my way as I twirl in my little black dress. ***I vote for the lemon yellow number. This one is far too boring.***

I scoff without meaning to. "Fish, everyone knows a little black dress makes you stand out. Besides, men can't seem to resist them. They just love them. And seeing that Jasper is a man, he will love it by proxy. I hope." I blow out a quick breath as I look into the full-length mirror in my bedroom.

Mistletoe and Holly sit perched over the Christmas quilt strewn over my bed. Their fur seems to have grown three inches in the short time I've had them, and they really do look like a couple of balls of fluff with eyes.

It's the night of the double date debacle with Camila and Jordy, and I've tried on at least a dozen dresses trying to find the right one. Of course, it's freezing out and I'll have to wear a coat regardless, but once we get inside, I want to be the only girl Jasper sees.

I groan at the thought. "I can't believe I agreed to drag Camila on a date with Jasper and me. Face it, Jordy is nothing more than window dressing, and if Camila has her way, I will be, too."

Mistletoe belts out a sharp meow. ***Now, now, don't be so hard on yourself.***

Holly growls, ***You had no choice. The witch blackmailed you.***

"That is true," I say, dusting a little blush over my cheeks.

Fish gives a lazy mewl in my direction. ***Would it really be so bad if Jasper knew your secret? Sherlock and I were just discussing this afternoon how freeing it would be. And poor Sherlock has never been able to communicate with Jasper the way I've been able to communicate with you. He would love to do that.***

I twist my lips at the thought. "I know. But let's be honest. All of Sherlock's conversations could be summarized in one word—*bacon*."

The three little kittens let out a series of mewls as they laugh themselves into a *cat*niption.

Holly meows over at me, ***What would be the worst that could happen, Bizzy? What damage could this conniving Camila truly achieve?***

I take a deep breath as I ponder the possibility. "Honestly, I don't know that anyone could truly prove that I can read minds. Not if I keep denying it, anyway." Jasper blinks through my mind with those stunning gray eyes and that face that commands the attention of any and every female. "The very worst that could happen is that Camila gets her way—I lose Jasper." I shudder at the thought. "I guess if he really wanted to be with her again I couldn't stop him. Unlike Camila, I would never want to force someone to be with me. But I'll admit, it kills me to imagine him with anyone else. Of course, I want him to be happy, but what I'd really like is for him to be happy with me."

Fish lets out a mighty roar. ***He'd be a fool to let you go.***

Why do I get the feeling tonight will put any foolishness Jasper might have in him to the test?

The Station is located on the east side of Cider Cove just above the inn and boasts of vast ocean views no matter where you're seated. It's dimly lit inside where elegantly dressed women and men abound everywhere you look. There's easy music filtering in through the speakers and a small dance floor up front where couples seem to migrate. And I can't help but notice that every single woman here is wearing a nearly identical little black dress.

Perfect. In an effort to stand out, I look as if I'm just another witch in the coven.

Jasper pulls me in, and the intoxicating scent of his cologne permeates my senses.

Bizzy Baker is what dreams are made of. Man. What are we doing here again? We should be at my place. Her place. Any place but the same place as Camila Ryder.

A smile floats to my lips just hearing his thought.

Jasper looks arresting tonight, shockingly handsome, actually. We've enjoyed a few fancy nights out before, but there's something about the dark pinstripe suit and his silver tie that only seems to accentuate his glowing eyes. It sends me to another headspace entirely. And as dashing as he is, a part of me wonders if he's turned up the volume on his good looks because he knew his ex would be here. Silly, I know.

"Come here." A side-lying dimple ignites in his cheek as he pulls me close. "You look amazing tonight. I'm pretty sure it's illegal to look this good in these parts—in any parts. Good thing I've got a pair of handcuffs on me. I'm this close to hauling you in."

"Oh, really? Because that suit with that devilish grin of yours has me thinking I need to make a citizen's arrest." A tiny giggle bubbles through me. "And thank you for the kind, yet quasi-threatening, words." I give a little wink. "Feel free to make good on any and all threats." I can think of worse things than being hauled out of a fancy restaurant in handcuffs—like a dinner date with his ex.

He steals a quick kiss and makes it linger. "I say no appetizers, straight to the meal, no dessert, and we ditch them as soon as possible."

"No dessert? You are a monster tonight." A dark laugh strums through me.

His lids hood low as a wicked smile crests on his lips. "I didn't say anything about skipping it. In fact, I think we should indulge all we want. In private."

"Perfect. We'll raid the café before heading to my place. That way I can pick up some bacon for Sherlock." I bite down playfully over my lip. “And I think there might be a few gingerbread whoopie pies in it for you and me.”

“Sounds sinfully delicious.” ***And what I have planned for her later is pretty sinful, too.*** He wraps his arms around me tightly. “I was beginning to think you like my dog a little better than you like me.”

“It’s a fine line—some might even call it a tie.”

A cloud of sugary perfume ensconces us, and I swear on all that is holy, I sense the presence of evil.

Someone clears their throat from behind and we turn to find Camila and Jordy looking stunning and dapper. Okay, fine. Camila is beyond stunning in a bright red dress. And in a sea of onyx gowns she looks like a—well, a devil ready to spear her victim with that pointed tail of hers.

Relax, Bizzy. She tightens that smile over her face. ***You’re snarling.***

Jasper straightens. “Camila. Jordy.” He openly frowns a moment. “Let’s take a seat.” ***And get this the hell over with.***

A waitress seats us at a table. An adorable petite blonde who keeps glancing back at Jasper as if she’s never seen a man before, at least not one like this.

Good Lord up in heaven, she muses. ***Where has this hunk of muscles been hiding out? I’d better get my number ready. Something tells me a man***

of his caliber needs more than one woman to keep him on his toes. He's too gorgeous for words.

My mouth falls open as Jasper holds my seat out for me.

"Thank you," I say before shooting a look to the wily waitress. "It's nice to have a man who cares about the little things like pulling out a chair. Of course, I do my best to keep him on his toes. He *is* too gorgeous for words."

The smile glides right off her face as her eyes enlarge. ***Wow, it's as if she just read my mind. My mother is right. I am an open book. Geez, she can probably see the fact I'm attracted to him written all over my face. Let's hope she's not in charge of the tip. But in the event she is, I'm not even looking at her date for the rest of the night. Message received.***

Good. Now to pass the message along to the other she-devil among us.

The waitress passes out the menus before taking off, and we all take a moment to peruse them.

Jordy leans in, looking perfectly handsome with his hair slicked back and clean-shaven face. His dark hair and blue eyes are a nice combination, and I hope Camila appreciates him on just about any level. I hate the fact she's using him. And she is doing just that. Lucky for Jordy, he's not a one-woman man. And considering he's already made his way through half the women in Maine, little does Camila know she's just another notch on his belt.

"So Bizzy"—Jordy leans my way—"Camila told me on the ride over that your mom is being investigated." He shakes his head at Jasper. "I can promise, you're barking up the wrong tree."

Jasper lets out a quick chuckle. "I've spent my time barking up plenty of wrong trees." He glances to Camila. ***Case in point.*** "I can assure you, talking to Ree is simply a part of the process."

I glower over at Camila a moment. It would figure she fills her spare time dragging my mother through the murderous mud. Of course, she mentioned it to Jordy.

It's as if she's equally obsessed with me as she is Jasper.

I give a quick glance around the place for the other thorn in my side I enlisted to make a guest appearance, but Mackenzie Woods is nowhere to be found.

Figures. If I can count on Mack for anything, it's to let me down in grand fashion.

"Camila." I force a tight smile. "How is that kitchen remodel coming?" I'm beginning to wonder if it even exists. That's the renovating malfeasance she cited for needing a place at the inn to begin with.

She belts out a biting laugh. ***You don't hide anything, do you, Bizzy Baker? You no more want me at the inn than I want to be there. But then again, you are hiding something, aren't you?***

She clears her throat. "I'll be just a few more weeks. Unless, of course, another thing goes wrong. With the way things have been going for me lately, I may as well change my name to Bad Luck Ryder." She purses her lips as she looks to Jasper for sympathy.

I've got a couple of names I'd like to call her.

Jordy nods her way as if he were genuinely interested. "I'll swing by your place and take a look at what's going on. I'll talk to the contractor with you if you want."

"Oh, Jordy," she coos as she takes up his hand. "I would love that. You have no idea how lucky I feel to have a big, strong man around for a change."

For a change? Jasper sits up a notch. ***What the heck does she think I was?***

I scowl over at her.

Great. Her ridiculous plan is working. And the fact Jasper isn't onto her ego-inspired coo is worrisome to me.

Not that I care what she thinks about me. He takes up my hand and gives it a squeeze. ***I'm no stranger to Camila's head games. She can have at the poor guy drooling next to her. I'm more than happy***

where I am. In fact, Camila better get an eyeful, because if I have my way, Bizzy and I aren't going anywhere. I'm talking marriage, kids. He glances my way. ***Come to think of it, I wonder if Bizzy wants kids, or even likes kids?***

"Jordy"— I perk to life—"remember when we were kids, how much fun we had when our parents drove us out to Pine Peak to throw snowballs at one another? I can't wait to do that with my own children one day."

Jasper shifts in his seat. ***I swear, sometimes it's like she's reading my mind.***

Good Lord, not the direction I wanted to head in.

A nervous laugh titters from me. "Jordy and I grew up together," I say to Camila. "So how about you, Camila? Kids? Marriage? Jordy's been waiting to be a dad for as long as I can remember."

Jordy shoots a look my way. ***Why do I get the feeling she's trying to upsell me?***

Camila gives a long blink. "I'm taking my time in that arena. I've always said two point five kids is the goal. Jasper wants an entire brood. I hope you're ready for that, Bizzy. Have you had the big talk about kids and marriage?"

My lips part as I look to Jasper. "No, I guess we haven't."

"Oh, I'm sorry." Camila chirps like an unwanted bird. "I guess I was assuming you were farther along in your relationship than you are. Well, once the two of you get serious, I'm sure you'll cover all the bases. Jordy and I have already discussed those things." She wrinkles her nose at Jasper. "You know me, I like to keep on top of all the important things. I spoke to your mother this morning, and she was just lamenting the fact she doesn't have grandchildren yet. We're going to the final fitting of her gown tomorrow afternoon. Ella is coming, too." She nods to Jordy. "Ella is Jasper's sister. We're like family. Of course, you'll be my guest at the wedding. Gwyn and Nathan have settled on the inn after all."

Settled? I roll my eyes at that one.

Jordy shakes his head. "What do you think, Bizzy? Your dad and his mother? That's pretty crazy, right?"

"Not as crazy as my mother and his brother." I wince over at Jasper. "Or my sister and his other brothers. Sorry about that."

Jordy laughs. "The two of you are practically family already."

Camila's expression sours just as the waitress comes by and we put in our orders.

Jordy and Jasper talk about the sheriff's department and work in general until our meals come and we bask in a few brief minutes of silence while we do our best to inhale a surf and turf dinner that costs more than what we charge for a room at the inn for an entire week—or just about.

Camila leans my way. "A little birdie told me that you've got an uncanny way of reading people." She cinches a dark smile. ***That's right, Bizzy. I'm unafraid. Tonight is the night you tell Jasper that you're not sure about a future with him. After all, you still have feelings for your ex-husband Jordy here.*** Her brows hike a notch. ***He bored me with the details of your Vegas shenanigans. Eloping while hopped up on hard liquor? How very original of you.***

Jordy gives a wistful shake of the head. "You're not kidding. Sometimes it feels as if Bizzy is prying right into my mind."

Jasper nods. "She's intuitive. That must be why hospitality is her calling."

"That's right." I sit up, thrilled to have Jasper hand me an easy out. Heck, I think I can ride with that excuse for the next seventy years. Hey? I really am thinking about marriage with Jasper. "I've always been good at reading people."

"Really?" Camila's brows hike a notch. "What am I thinking now?" ***Don't think for a minute that you've gotten away with something here. You might***

think you've bested me, but I have an ace up my sleeve you will never see coming.

I clear my throat. "You're thinking how lucky you feel to be so welcomed in Cider Cove. Not only are you on good terms with your ex, but you have a new man by your side. And just in time for the holidays. There's nothing like a little romance in time for Christmas Eve." I give Jasper's fingers a squeeze and he brings my hand to his lips and kisses the back of it.

Camila's lips curl at the sight. ***My, my, you are about to break his heart something awful. I'll make sure to have the rebound ready in the wings.***

I grunt at the thought and Jasper lets go of my hand.

"I'm sorry." He blinks back, surprised by my not-so-silent outburst.

"Believe me"—I don't hesitate taking up his hand once again—"you did nothing wrong."

He's about to respond when something catches his eye and he lets out a heavy sigh instead.

And here he is.

I look up to see Mackenzie and Leo holding one another close as they sway to the music on the dance floor. And if I'm not mistaken, Mack is slowly leading them in this direction. I almost feel sorry for Leo getting pulled into his ex's drama—*almost* being the operative word. None of us would be in this perilous predicament if it weren't for Leo's inability to keep a secret.

Mack pretends to do a double take our way before walking over with Leo trailing behind her like a naughty child. She's donned the requisite little black dress, and I make a mental note to pay attention to Fish's opinions when it comes to fashion next time.

Mack growls out a short-lived laugh. "Well, well, the gang's all here."

The entire lot of us exchanges polite hellos, with the exception of Camila who looks as if she just met up with a freight train while looking at her ex.

Leo takes a breath as he glances my way. ***Why do I get the feeling this is no accident, Bizzy?***

Because you're as intuitive as I am. I make a face. ***Mack wants Camila out of town as much as I do. But I think we both know I've got more at stake than she does.***

He rocks back on his heels. ***Great. And you think the two of you can make this miracle happen? Godspeed because I'll be the last person to stand in your way.***

Mackenzie gives Jasper an approving once-over. "Detective Wilder, any updates on the latest homicide to rock Cider Cove?"

"Nothing new outside of what the media covered."

"So it's true?" Mackenzie looks mildly affronted. "We have another killer on the loose? I'm not liking the way the homicides are racking up, Detective. Please tell the sheriff I'm putting him on notice."

"Duly noted." Jasper looks my way. "How about we hit the dance floor?" ***And then we hit the exit.*** His brows hike a notch.

"You just read my mind."

We hit the dance floor as if escaping an inferno, and no sooner am I in the warmth of Jasper's arms than I spot a woman with a long blonde ponytail dressed in a gold glittering dress heading to the door with an older gentleman who happens to be grinning from ear-to-ear. Just looking at her sends all sorts of alarm bells off inside me. I recognize her from the night of the murder.

That's Trixie Jolly-Golightly, Lincoln Brooks' girlfriend! And if I'm not mistaken, it looks as if she's on a date.

I'm about to tell Jasper exactly who she is, but I'm half-afraid he'll try to talk me out of what inevitably comes next.

"Jasper, I'll be right back," I say as I untangle myself from him, my eyes never leaving that glittering woman quickly heading to the exit.

Jasper steps in close. “Where are you headed?”

“Restroom,” I call out as I thread my way through the crowd, but no sooner do I get to the entry than it’s too late. They’ve disappeared into the night.

What would Trixie be doing out painting the town red with another man while her boyfriend lies cold in the morgue?

My mind is filled with half-baked theories as I make my way back to Jasper, and just as I’m about to reach him, I spot another woman in his arms—a laughing Camila Ryder.

Mackenzie looks fit to kill as she bustles my way. “Would you explain to me how running away from the man you profess you’d like to keep helps the situation? Do you see what happens when you turn your back?”

Camila catches my eye. ***That’s right, Bizzy. It’s all over between you and Jasper tonight. Or else, phase two of Operation Get Rid of Bizzy Baker is set into motion.***

Leo heads their way and taps Jasper on the shoulder, and soon he’s dancing with his disgruntled looking ex, whispering something into Camila’s ear that causes her to shoot daggers my way.

I bet he’s telling her he knows about her threats.

Wonderful. I’m sure that will make everything better.

Mack gives a silent huff. “Watch and learn.”

She takes off and evicts Camila from her man as if she were flicking a tick off of him. But I think we all know it's not Leo's blood she's after.

It's Jasper she wants to take a bite out of. And she's willing to knock down any and everyone in her way—namely me.

Jasper plunks down a chunk of bills onto the table and we hightail it all the way back to my cottage and get straight to dessert.

Camila isn't winning this war.

And Trixie Jolly-Golightly isn't getting away with murder.

But for the next few hours, I wipe both of them out of my mind as I enjoy every delicious bite of what's on my plate.

10

I didn't do it.

Who in their right mind would have?

Of course, I didn't break up with Jasper. The idea is beyond ridiculous. If anything, I'm breaking up with Camila and her crazy notion that she can control me via blackmail.

As if.

What did I think would come of that pricey steak and lobster dinner? And believe me when I say Jasper lost a month's worth of paychecks over that fiasco. But in Jordy's defense, by the time the bill arrived, he was trying his best to peel his ditzy date off of Leo.

I'm not sure why Mackenzie is convinced that Camila is after her man. I'm certainly not buying it. Nope. Camila the con artist is strictly after my man. And after those heated kisses Jasper and I exchanged back at my cottage, he officially qualifies as mine in every single way.

Long story short. I'm done with Crazy Camila.

After a long day at the inn, I decide to gather up my menagerie and head down to Candy Cane Lane. Of course, as soon as Georgie got wind that I was headed to see the holiday lights once again, she quickly dove into the passenger's seat of my car. And since Macy was present at the time, she promptly followed us over in the event there would be handsome men schnockered off eggnog looking to have a little fun under the mistletoe—her words, not mine.

Outside, the wind is biting and it's icy enough to snow right now if it wanted to. Good thing we've bundled up within an inch of our scarf-loving lives. If I weren't wearing gloves, my fingers would freeze solid and break right off.

It takes almost ten minutes for Georgie and me to pull out the cat stroller and load Fish, Mistletoe, and Holly inside.

Fish makes herself at home in the center of the plush seat, while the younger kittens snuggle up on either side of her like a pair of fuzzy little bookends.

Bizzy—Fish yowls—***make sure to spend extra time near the house with the giant dog. They have bushels of catnip out front.***

"Giant dog?" I try to recall which house that might be just as Mistletoe yelps.

She means the wicked witch's house. They had that giant moose milling around, chewing on the bushes.

"Oh!" I say as Georgie comes around the side of the car with Sherlock on a leash, his cumbersome cone bumping into any and everything. "You mean the reindeer at the Bronsons' home." I smile over at Georgie. "Fish is convinced the Bronsons are growing catnip."

Georgie grunts out a laugh. "Oh, they're growing something—murderous deceit. We'll have to investigate, my furry little friend. We will have to investigate." She gives Sherlock a quick pat on the back. "How long does this old guy have to wear the cone of shame? Other dogs are beginning to point and laugh. I saw a Pekingese at the inn turn his smushed little nose up at our favorite fuzzy pooch." Sherlock moans and Georgie falls hook, line, and sinker for those big brown eyes. "Don't you worry, big boy. I've got a pocket full of bacon for you, and ain't nobody going to laugh and point while you have your fill of pork belly."

Hear that? Sherlock lets out a sharp bark. ***I get to fill my porky belly with bacon! But before I forget, I'd like the record to show, the cone of shame is***

nothing I'm interested in pursuing as a long-term goal.

A tiny laugh bubbles from me. "Sherlock, where did you learn such sophisticated language when it comes to goal setting?"

When Jasper talks to himself, I pay attention. You should hear the things he says about you.

"Oh, I do." I give a little wink as the six of us start our stroll down Candy Cane Lane.

The sun has just set and every house is lit up like a jewel, shimmering in all of its holiday splendor. There are more wreathes, oversized toy soldiers, blowup snowmen and Grinches than should ever be legal in a one-mile vicinity. The carolers are out in full force, the carriage strung with twinkle lights is already making its way up the street, and every corner has a hot cocoa or cookie stand. Believe me when I say those fresh baked chocolate chip cookies smell divine.

Georgie smacks me as we come upon the Bronsons' house. "Get a load of that."

She points over to a familiar looking trio and we quickly make our way over.

It's Macy, Emmie, and Jamison, Jasper's brother who looks hauntingly like Jasper himself. I swear on all that is holy, Gwyneth had triplets years apart. Each Wilder brother looks like a carbon copy of the other. And, of course, their sister is another look-alike in female skin.

"Hey, Emmie." I pull my best friend in. Her dark hair is up in a messy bun, she's wearing a bright red wool coat that hugs her figure, and her eyes sparkle with approval at the man in our midst. I say a quick hello to Jamison and he flashes that all too familiar smile my way.

"Nice to see you, Bizzy," he says. "I take it my brother is hard at work. That's Jasper for you."

I nod. "There's a new case he's working on."

Macy looks over at him from over the steaming cup of cider in her hands. "Bizzy found the body. It's a new game she likes to play called Find the Corpse. She's thinking of going pro."

"Very funny," I flatline to my sister before shifting my attention to Jamison. "I plan on leaving all of the corpses to the pros—namely Jasper."

Jamison chuckles. "Well, if he wasn't dating you, I'm sure he'd arrest you. It's odd that you're always at ground zero when a body turns up."

Macy leans in. "Bizzy is our resident serial killer."

We all share a warm laugh—some laughing more than others—and my laugh sounds more like a threat.

Jamison nods my way. "I guess we'll see you tomorrow night at Maximus." A trace of a smile glides off his face. “Our parents seem dead set on going through with this thing.”

Georgie grunts, “This *thing* is called love, Jamison. Get with the program. You can be an ageist elitist all you want, but passion lives well past fifty.” She gives a little wink his way.

Emmie takes up his hand. “Speaking of passion, we’d better be going. This is our first official date.” She bites down on her lip as she makes wild eyes my way. “Wish me luck!”

Jamison laughs as he pulls her in close. “I think I’m the lucky one around here.”

Macy coos as they head on down the street.

“Was that weird?” I whisper her way once they leave.

“No.” She frowns over at me. “Why would that be weird?”

“Because you cycled through him.” I nod without extrapolating on the innuendo.

Macy is quick to wave me off. “Cycling through them is how I test them out. He’s a good one—just not the one for me.”

Georgie follows Sherlock as he leads her to the bushes in front of the Bronsons’ home.

The front lawn is layered with white batting, and underneath that there’s a layer of blue twinkle lights that gives it a magical appeal—and I can't help but notice it looks exactly the way Lincoln's front lawn looked on the night he was killed. It wasn't this way the other night. I guess Lincoln was right when he said Dexter stole all his ideas.

And seated on the golden throne at the Bronsons' is a well-dressed Santa, and there are only a few kids in line, seeing that it's still early.

"Ooh." Macy fluffs her short blonde mane. "I need to get a picture with Santa."

I'm about to tell her how adorable I think that is when she lifts a hand my way.

"Don't look at me like that, Bizzy. Everyone knows it's good luck to sit on a man wearing a red velvet suit at least once a year."

"At *least*." Georgie honks out a laugh while elbowing my sister in the ribs.

"I'm not sitting on a stranger's lap tonight. And if that Santa is who I think it is, I'm pretty sure it would be the opposite of good luck," I say, squinting over at the man in the big red suit, and sure enough I see it's Dexter Bronson himself.

Georgie lifts a finger my way. "If I were you, I'd buy Jasper a red velvet suit just in case. Macy is right. You've made quite the hobby out of finding dead bodies. I think you need to do everything you can to get your hands—and maybe a few other body parts—on for some good luck."

"I'm not sure I believe in luck," I say as I glance across the street and note that all of Lincoln's decorations are lit up. The fake snow on the front lawn is a little askew and the throne is barren, save for a few families taking their own pictures around it. I suppose Lincoln has the whole thing set on timers. At least his home will be appreciated one last holiday season.

A light goes on in one of the upstairs windows and immediately snatches my attention.

Huh.

I wonder if Trixie is home?

Fish meows until Georgie opens the mesh liner to the stroller and all three cats are happily craning their necks at the bushes before us.

Is this it? Fish cries out happily. ***Is this the catnip farm?***

"Georgie, Fish wants to know if there's any catnip around." I point to the oversized bush with long dagger-like leaves.

"Heavens no." Georgie tosses her hands up and quickly zips the cats back up in the event they decide to hop on out an indulge on the first leaf they see. "That's oleander. It's a death trap for cats and people alike. None for you either, Sherlock."

A thought comes to me. "Georgie? Maybe you could hop in line with Macy. I bet all the animals would love to get their pictures taken with Santa."

Sherlock barks and the cats mewl, suddenly taken with the idea of sitting on a red velvet suit themselves.

Georgie leans in, following my gaze. "Good idea, Bizzy. You go across the street and break into old man Brooks' house and see if you can find a clue that will lead you to the killer."

"I'm not breaking in. That's illegal." Although, I don't think I'll have to stoop to breaking the law. Something tells me Trixie Jolly-Golightly just might act as my willing accomplice.

I make my way across the street, threading through the crowd all bundled in their scarves and matching mittens as white plumes blow from everyone's mouth and nostrils. It's supposed to dip below freezing tonight once again, and there's a storm pushing through, so the chances of snow are in our favor.

Lincoln Brooks' home looks a little more sorrowful up close than it did from across the street. The wind has left the cotton batting snow curled up on one side and a string of white lights dangle from the eaves down to the lawn, creating a rather sad line right in front of the living room window.

I make my way up the porch and give a few quick knocks. I can hear the sound of something shifting from inside as footsteps draw in this direction.

"*Hello*?" a friendly female voice calls from inside before the door swings open, revealing a woman with her hair in a bun, dressed in a red silk blouse and houndstooth trousers. I can't help but note she looks office chic with her oversized tortoise-framed glasses. I recognize her from the night of the murders. She has the same open face and same friendly eyes that I remember.

"Julia?" I blink back. "It's me, Bizzy Baker. I was here the night of the—" I stop shy of saying *murder*.

"Oh, that's right." She widens the door and motions for me to come inside. "Nice to see you again, Bizzy. I was just in the office, closing out some accounts the best way I knew how. You work at the Country Cottage Inn, right? I remember hearing about you and those awful murders. I don't know what's happening in this sleepy town. It's just terrible."

"I agree with you," I say as I cautiously step in. "You mentioned you were his secretary, right?" I ask as she closes the door behind me, dampening the sound of the revelry and it's a welcome relief to my ears.

"Yup." She ticks her head at the thought. "And sadly, I really am out of a job. Believe me, the reality stings."

"Sorry about that."

It's warm and toasty inside and the lights are all on downstairs, giving the home a cheery appeal. There's a Christmas tree in the corner strung with bright white lights, and I suppose that's set on a timer, too. I feel terrible that Lincoln isn't around to enjoy the holiday he seemed to love so much.

I clear my throat. "I was just across the street with my friends and I saw a light on. I was thinking I might catch Trixie here. Is she home?"

Julia all but rolls her eyes. "Are you kidding? She hasn't been back since the night she killed him." She pulls a pin from her bun and her hair dislodges loosely around her shoulders.

"You think she killed him?"

"You think she didn't?" There's an amused undertone in her voice. "I talked to the sheriff's department and they think he was poisoned. I've been telling Lincoln for the last solid year that Trixie was trying to poison him with her cooking. It looks as if she got him with the eggnog instead." She gives a little shrug. "You want to take a seat? Or you can come with me into the office and we can talk in there. I only have a few more things to button up before I call it a night, and I'd appreciate the company. Being alone in this place has always given me the creeps, but even more so now that he's gone."

"Absolutely. I'll head to the office with you." Something in me soars and I can't help but think I've won the investigative lottery. I follow along as we make our way across the hardwood floors, past cozy rooms filled with oversized furniture, a dark stained table and chairs in the dining room. We pass the kitchen, which looks like a modern marvel with its stainless appliances and expansive island. The kitchen is spacious enough to have a working restaurant in this room alone.

Finally, we make our way down a small hall and into an office about the size of my entire cottage. There are Bankers Boxes stacked on one another in the corner and a large steel desk with two computers sitting side by side, both lit up and running.

Julia plops down in the seat in front of one and begins clicking away at the keyboard.

"You can take a seat if you want. I'm just logging out." She motions to a stack of books in a Bankers Box. "Lincoln was big on horticulture. You can take any of those. He was about to have me send them to the library for donation."

I peruse the small pile of hardbacks and paperbacks on gardening. *The Necrotic Botanist, Holistic Horticulture, Life in the Garden.*

“If you don’t mind, I know my friend Georgie will go wild over these,” I say, picking up the first three.

“Please take the entire thing. You’ll save me a trip.”

“Great. I will.” I pull the Bankers Box to the side.

“I’m letting all of his fellow investors, clients, friends, and anyone who I think will care know that he’s passed away. He didn’t have any kids, or family to speak of, and I doubt Trixie will be springing for an expensive funeral for him. I’m afraid these emails will be as close to a memorial service as he’ll get.”

“Poor guy. Do you think maybe Mary Beth will want to take care of the arrangements?”

She shoots me a look as a tiny laugh sputters from her. “Doubtful. If anything, she’s the next person I’d blame his death on, right after Trixie. I mean, it’s obvious both women hated him.”

“That’s probably true on Mary Beth’s part.” I didn’t sense any sorrow when I spoke to her the other day. She was cold and unfeeling. Heck, I might just bump her to the top of the suspect list.

“It’s true for sure,” Julia says as the computer in front of her darkens and she moves on to the next one. “I called the Trident Society and they said they'll collect him from the morgue and cremate him for a nominal fee. I still have access to the small slush fund I used to pay incidentals with. There's only about six hundred dollars in there, but I'm sure that will be enough to take care of everything for him." The second computer grows dark as she spins in her seat.

"Julia, what makes you so sure Trixie did it? I would love for whoever did this to get caught."

"Oh, they will." ***Trixie isn't that good at hiding.*** "And it will be Trixie." She shakes her head. "At least I'm fairly certain of it. She threatened him a time or two right in front of me. I let the sheriff's deputy who was interviewing me know that. Trixie and Lincoln had a big blowout in the living room two weeks ago and she said something to the effect of 'you can't make me do it.' They were both charged and heated. I thought they were going to come to blows, so I crept out of there. I was actually hiding in the kitchen because I didn't want to embarrass them, but I felt like I might be needed to stop something. You know, in the event they started throwing vases at each other. Anyway, she was really coming at him. She said she'd end him if he ever thought of threatening her that way again."

"What do you think he was threatening her over?" My heart leaps into my throat, because suddenly it feels as if the layers to the mystery are about to be stripped away.

Julia picks up a stack of mail and shoves it into a bag.

She takes a moment to grimace my way. "You don't know much about Trixie, do you?"

I shake my head. "I was actually hoping to extend my condolences and see if she needs anything."

A sharp laugh belts from her. "Oh, she doesn't. A woman like Trixie knows exactly how to get her needs met while meeting the needs of others. She worked at some strip club out in Edison for years. Eventually, she aged out of dancing and started taking on personal clients."

"Clients?" My cheeks heat because I have a feeling I know exactly what kind of clients she's referring to.

"Yup. And I know exactly what you're thinking because I'm thinking it, too. Trixie once told me she just accepts payment for her *company*. And seeing that most of the men she chooses to keep company with are much older, that might be the case. I guess Lincoln wanted to keep her to himself exclusively. I'm not sure why she wouldn't oblige him. I mean, they took trips all around the world, ate at fancy restaurants almost every night, and he even bought out a diamond mine to outfit her with sparkling jewels. Okay, so that might be a slight exaggeration, but he was very good to her. All he wanted was some exclusivity. I think he wanted to believe it was real—that a woman like Trixie could love him." She takes a deep breath as she cinches her purse over her shoulder. "But it all came to a head," she says, helping me pick up the box full of books I'm taking for Georgie before leading the way out of the office and flicking off the lights. "She wanted her freedom, and he wanted to own her. He could be very possessive. But he was vibrant. Far more than those other men Trixie showed me pictures of. I guess she liked things status quo. If they pin her for this murder, she's going to have a serious change of lifestyle in prison."

We make our way to the living room and Julia holds the door open for me as I step out with my Bankers Box full of books. A few of the women minding their children on the lawn do a double take my way.

"I must look like a vulture coming out of a dead man's house with a box of his things," I whisper to Julia.

She titters a small laugh. "You're helping a friend out. And that friend would be me. If you're still looking to offer your condolences to Trixie, she likes to hang out at the City Limits Bar and Grill. I think it's in downtown Seaview."

"Great. I'll actually be in Seaview tomorrow night for a family dinner at Maximus. Maybe I'll stop by and see if I can spot her."

"She'll be easy to spot, all right. She likes to wear glittery gowns when she's out trolling for men. She thinks it makes her look *classy*." She says *classy* with air quotes as we make our way down the porch. "I live in the carriage house in the back. If you need anything at all, stop by again. I'll be hanging around for another week or so until I can get something lined up. I applied for a job down in South Carolina, and I'm crossing my fingers I get it. I just love the South, and the weather is to die for."

A dark laugh rumbles through me as we part ways. "On a frosty night like tonight, I'm tempted to join you." I stop short. "Oh, Julia? There's a benefit and silent auction coming up for needy families at the inn. It's the night before Christmas Eve, and if you don't have any plans, please come as my guest. I'd love for one of your last memories in Cider Cove to be a good one."

"Thank you, Bizzy. I will do that."

And they've all been good memories so far. She warms herself with her arms as she heads for the back.

Nice lady. Too bad Trixie isn't a nice lady.

But is she a killer?

I'll do my best to find out exactly that tomorrow night.

11

The very next morning, the inn is bustling with out-of-towners ready to stay through the holidays as they visit local friends and family. It's so cozy at the inn this time of year. I wish the season would last forever. I spent the morning hanging stockings above the enormous stone fireplace in the grand room with each employee's name written across the front in gold glitter paint. The whole inn is lit up with the scent of those gingerbread whoopie pies the Country Cottage Café is baking nonstop. And just a few minutes ago, the Sugar Plum Tree Lot delivered those evergreens I ordered the other day and the entire front of the inn holds the scent of a fresh cut pine forest.

Jordy laughs as he shakes his head my way. "Bizzy, you've got enough to put two trees in every room."

"That sounds like my kind of decorating," I say as I do my best to cinch my coat. It's freezing out here—*literally* and we finally have a sheet of white frost that's sticking to the ground. All of Cider Cove looks like the inside of a snow globe with the trees surrounding the inn dusted with snow and the roofs of the cottages covered in a sheet of white. Sherlock strides up beside me as I make my way to the delivery truck.

Are the cookies here, Bizzy? Are the cookies here? That's a big truck! That means there are lots of cookies.

A laugh bubbles from me. "I hate to break it to you, Sherlock, but the cookie exchange isn't until tomorrow."

A hard groan comes from him, but his disappointment is short-lived as he licks the side of a rock and eats the frost right off it.

It tastes like ice cream! Fish, come quick! He barks as he speeds back into the inn to spread the news to his furry friends no doubt.

I'm about to head back myself when Calvin St. James strides up in his well-worn jeans and black and red buffalo flannel. He wears an easy smile, and there's a warmth in his eyes you can't deny.

"Hi, Calvin!" I give a cheery wave. "You brought the whole forest," I tease.

He nods my way. "I thought I'd throw in a few extra. You are, after all, hosting the Christmas charity event."

"Thank you," I say. "The more trees, the merrier." I look to Jordy. "Go ahead and set them up wherever you can fit them. We have boxes and boxes of twinkle lights to decorate them with. They're going to look beautiful."

Jordy gives me a mock salute. "You got it, boss." He takes off and helps the men off-load the trees from the back of the delivery truck.

Calvin nods my way. "Nice to see you again, Bizzy."

"Likewise. And this is more Christmas cheer than I expected. I just want you to know I'm grateful for every last branch. Thank you, Calvin." Julia crosses my mind. "I hear Lincoln's secretary is trying to help contact everyone he's done business with. Have you heard from her yet?"

"She called me a few days ago. I told her not to worry about anything. I contacted everyone Lincoln and I were dealing with and asked them to forward any future inquiries my way." ***Now that Lincoln isn't around to complicate things, I might actually turn a profit for a change.***

Interesting. He virtually had the same thought the last time we met. At least he's consistent.

"Good," I say. "I'm glad you spoke with her."

He ticks his head to the side. “Julia’s a good person. She always had everything lined up and squared away for him. She was probably the best thing that’s ever happened to Lincoln. Now if he could have only had a romantic connection with her, he might still be alive. But Lincoln always did like his women with a slice of danger on the side. It looks like this last one was a bit too dangerous.”

That’s two strikes for Trixie. It looks like Julia and Calvin can agree she is capable of murder.

“Well, I hope the sheriff’s department makes an arrest soon.” I warm my arms with my hands. “I think we could all rest a little easier this holiday season if they did. It’s chaotic enough without a killer running loose.”

He glances skyward a moment. “Or maybe that’s what the killer wanted—to throw a little more chaos into an already chaotic season.”

Now there’s a thought. “Intentional or not, this season certainly comes with its distractions.” And one distraction after another might just help someone get away with murder. “What do I owe you?” Calvin has already made it clear he’s donating these to the inn, but I would love to pay him for the time and trouble.

He holds up his hands as if it were a stickup. “I meant what I said. The trees are a gift. You can’t stop me. I’ll be back for the event. See you in less than two weeks. And as it turns out, I'll be bringing a guest, but I still need to buy her a ticket. You didn't sell out, did you?"

"Actually, the ticket sales are run through the city, but I have a handful to give out. Wait right here. I'll run in and grab one. You can't stop me," I tease as I head back up the cobblestone path that leads to the entry.

A couple of well-dressed men enter the inn before I can get there, and by the time I step inside, they're already on their way to the café.

"Grady," I whisper to my dark-haired coworker that the women around here often refer to as an Irish god. He's a few years younger than me, fresh out of college, and he helps run the front desk with me. "Who were those men?"

He casts a glance in their direction. "I don't know. But they were looking to speak with you."

"Me? I guess I should go see what they want. Would you do me a favor and give the man by the truck outside a couple of those spare tickets to the Christmas charity event?" I head over to the café, and just as I'm about to enter, I spot both Leo and Jasper speaking to the two men in long wool coats. One of them looks to be holding up a badge of some sort.

Leo catches my eyes but doesn't move his head as if he didn't want to get caught in the endeavor.

Bizzy, go to your cottage and stay inside. Get ready for the big dinner tonight. I'll make sure this gets taken care of. Whatever you do, don't come out.

That sounds ominous.

Leo, what's going on? I take a step in their direction and he holds up a finger.

Bizzy, go home and lock the door. If anyone knocks, do not answer. Jasper and I have this. We'll talk tonight.

One of the men glances in my direction, and I quickly step out of his line of vision. I pivot on my heels and collect Sherlock, Fish, and the kittens while asking Grady to man the fort.

I head straight for my cottage and lock the door behind me.

Something tells me Camila's vengeance is far more dangerous than I could have ever suspected.

As soon as night falls, I'm off to Seaview to have dinner with all of my favorite people, and Gwyneth.

Maximus Seafood and Steakhouse is located on a prime strip of real estate just across from the boardwalk with sweeping views of the Atlantic.

I'll admit, all afternoon I've been more than nervous about what news Leo might have for me. Jasper went straight to his office after the bizarre encounter and said he'd meet me at the restaurant. He didn't say a word about the incident.

Having all but admitted to Camila that I can read people's thoughts is proving to be the grave error I knew it would be. Of course, I may have committed another grave error on the way over, which was telling Georgie that we had a couple of mystery men visit the inn this afternoon. Georgie's been spouting off theories ever since, and not all of them are comfortable to listen to.

"I don't think they're aliens from another planet," I whisper as we step inside the posh establishment owned by Jasper's brother. Not only is Maximus his brother's restaurant, but it bears his brother's moniker as well.

Georgie checks her face in the large-framed mirror hanging in the entry.

"Okay, so maybe they're not aliens looking to take you back to the mother planet. Maybe it's worse." She gasps and her eyes grow the size of hardboiled eggs as if she's just reached a hair-raising epiphany. "Maybe they think *you're* the alien!"

I give a slight nod. "That's exactly what I'm afraid of."

A waitress leads us through the dimly lit establishment, and I take in the well-polished look, the steel and dark wood décor, and the expansive bar that glitters with crystal chandeliers. We're led into a large banquet room in the back where cheery Christmas music is already filtering through the speakers, and I recognize most of the faces in the room. It's practically elbow-to-elbow in here. I can't believe my father and Gwyneth are having such a huge engagement party. It makes everything feel so real. But I still can't shake the feeling we're on a slippery slope. If my father decides he wants out of this marriage, the way he's decided he's wanted out of dozens of other marriages before this, I'm not too sure Jasper will be all that thrilled. I bet he'll rue the day he met me.

Georgie and I make the rounds saying hello to all of Jasper's brothers and his very pregnant sister, Ella.

"When are you due again?" I ask, taking in how beautiful she looks. Her skin glows like peaches and cream, and she's wearing a red A-line dress that accentuates her adorable baby bump.

"End of March, beginning of April. I'm rooting for March."

"That's right." I laugh. "That's exactly what you said at the harvest festival back in October. I bet you can't wait to hold that sweet baby in your arms."

"You have no idea how anxious I am." She pulls forth the man standing next to her. "This is my husband, Marcus. You probably met him at the art show a few weeks back." She leans toward Georgie. "He owns Westbrook Fishing Company. He hired me on as the clerk, and that's where it all began." She pats her belly, and we share a laugh.

Georgie and I exchange polite hellos with the muscular man by her side. He's bald and has a twinkle in his eyes when he smiles and tells us it's a pleasure to see us again.

We head off, and I spot my mother and Macy standing near a small bar set up in the room just for us. They're both dressed to the nines, each in their own version of a little black dress.

Macy holds up a glass filled with a glowing blue concoction. "Cocktails for the lucky ones, and mocktails for those of you who have to drive. Which will it be, Bizzy?"

"Mocktail, please. I'm driving—not to mention the inn is hosting Cider Cove's official cookie exchange bright and early tomorrow. Be sure to stop by. And come hungry," I say just as the crowd lights up with a cheer, and I look to the right to see my father and Gwyneth hamming it up with a real smooch of a kiss. “Boy, I wish I could make that mocktail a cocktail.”

Mom grunts, “You and me both, kid.”

I pull her in for a hug. “I can’t believe you came, Mom. You deserve a medal.”

“Not to worry. I have one. I’m here with my boyfriend, who happens to own the place.” No sooner does she get the words out than one of Jasper’s look-alikes wraps his arms around her from behind and dots her cheek with a kiss.

No matter how unnerving it looks, I must admit, it’s adorable to witness.

Macy groans as Maximus sweeps my mother off to give her a preview of the buffet.

“Why is it the good ones are always taken?” My sister laments as she takes a sip of her day-glow concoction. “And why are they taken by my mother?”

I glance to the left and see both Dalton and Jamison talking to Dad and Gwyneth. It’s eerie the way the Wilder men all look alike. A part of me is tempted to land one in a dark corner and land a heated kiss on his lips—now to find the *right* one.

“Macy, you can’t complain about Mom. You slept your way through two perfectly good Wilder brothers,” I tell her.

Macy scoffs at the truth bomb I just launched her way. "Details, details, Bizzy." She glances to Georgie. "Please tell my sister not all of us want to be tied down."

"I don't know"—Georgie takes another look at Dalton and Jamison—"I'd offer to tie myself up if I could get one of them to pay attention to me. I think you goofed this one, Macy. And you gave one away to Emmie. No takesies backsies." She wags a crooked finger at my sister. "If I were you, I'd make another pass at Dalton."

"Ha," I say. "Get it? Pass? He's a football coach. Good one, Georgie." I hold up a hand and she gives me a high five.

Macy knocks back the rest of her glowing drink before squinting their way once again.

"Fine." She hands me her empty glass, her eyes never leaving Dalton's direction. "I'll see if I can't score another touchdown before Christmas Eve." She snorts at the thought. "Who am I kidding? I'll be running one down the field tonight."

She takes off and Georgie heads for the bar.

I'm about to make my way over and congratulate the lucky couple when Camila swoops my way like an unwanted apparition.

"*Boo,*" she says it low with a measured giddiness in her voice. She's donned a blue velvet dress that hugs every last inch of her and glows around the edges as if it were backlit. Camila is a showstopper on an ordinary day, but at the moment she looks as if she could rouse the dead with her beauty. “I spoke to Jasper last night. We had another little heart-to-heart once he got home from your place.”

I blink back.

Jasper did stop by my place last night. We had dinner and he picked up Sherlock like he usually does. But by the time we had dinner and shared a few extra sweet kisses for dessert, it was almost midnight when he left.

She crimps a tight smile. “That’s right. Jasper and I shared some one-on-one time well into the wee hours of the morning. And from what I could gather, you didn’t break things off with him like we discussed.” She twitches her nose, her eyes brightening with the undeniable look of delight. “I’m just a teeny bit glad about it, too. I’m so eager to share phase two of my plan with you. It will be so much better to see the two of you implode rather than you letting him down without so much of a whimper.” Her shoulders bounce to her ears. “Stay tuned! I don’t want you to miss a thing.” She squints over at the bar. “You should try the poinsettia punch. It’s your father’s signature drink for the evening. I wonder what signature cocktails Jasper and I will have at our wedding?” She taps the side of her chin. “I’m sure you’ll see for yourself when the time comes. After all, we're all one big family now, aren't we?" She takes off and leaves me in the wake of her saccharin perfume.

Leo pops up, looking over me like a dark shadow, and all I can make out are the whites of his eyes.

I sigh up at him. "Is there a cocktail called A Cure for the Grinch? Because Camila needs a double helping. Leo, who were those men?"

His lips twitch as he glances to the door. "Jasper's here. He's on his way in. I think I'll let him tell you. I want your reaction to be genuine. Just know those men won't be back for a while."

Jasper appears through the door, dressed in a dark suit and a slick red tie that offsets his eyes and makes them look like twin lightning bolts.

"Bizzy, you look beautiful." His lids hood low and his lips curve at the tips. He wraps his arms around me and lands a light kiss to my lips. "Leo," he growls out his name like an insult. ***Granger just does not listen. I guess telling him to stay away from Bizzy wasn't enough. That's okay. I'll let my fist do the talking this time. I'll gift him a swollen eye for Christmas. That should do it.***

Leo's smile expands my way. "You are one lucky girl, Bizzy Baker. This guy right here has eyes only for you."

Jasper glowers as if he wasn't buying what Leo is selling.

"Jasper"—I step in close—"what did those men at the inn want this afternoon?"

He opens his mouth to answer just as my father and his mother descend upon us.

"Bizzy Bizzy!" Dad pulls me into a quick embrace as I congratulate both him and Gwyneth, and Jasper does the same. Leo offers his congratulations as well just as Mackenzie appears and whisks him off into the crowd.

Dad looks dapper in a gray suit and his usual cheery smile. And Gwyneth stuns in a gown that looks as if it's made of liquid silver.

Jasper takes a moment to examine them both. "It's coming down to the wire. You kids ready to do this?"

The four of us share a warm laugh.

Gwyneth hitches her thumb at my father. "Rumor has it, this guy is always up for a good wedding."

Dad nods, quick to admit it. "And don't worry about a thing. Both Dalton and Huxley are preparing the prenup."

Jasper twitches a brow. "Having two attorneys in the family will undoubtedly come in handy." ***I'm guessing we'll need them to unite for the divorce as well.***

Unfortunately, I think he's right.

I force a smile in Gwyneth's direction.

"Let me know if you need anything for the big day. I already have the Country Café ready to cater to the event."

A wedding on Christmas Eve of all days. There goes any hope of a small, family Christmas.

Speaking of family, I glance back, and sure enough I spot my brother talking to Macy.

"I have to say hello to Hux. I haven't seen him since Thanksgiving."

A crowd of friends quickly absorbs Dad and Gwyneth, so I link arms with Jasper, landing us before my brother and my sister. Huxley and I share the same dark hair and pale blue eyes. He's been married and divorced three times, no kids. I'm a little bit fearful he's stepping right into my father's shoes and is destined to have a string of divorces. I'd give anything if my sister and my brother could find what Jasper and I have.

"Huxley!" I dive over him with a firm embrace, and Jasper says hello to both him and Macy.

Hux growls over at Jasper, "I'd say I'm sorry about what's about to ensue with my father and your mother, but I think they're old enough to make their own mistakes." He looks to me. "Macy just told me Lincoln Brooks is dead and that Mom is a suspect." He glances to Jasper. "You're kidding me, right?"

Jasper takes a breath. "No, it's true. But she's as good as cleared." He sheds a quiet smile my way. "I have no reason to believe your mother was the one to spike Lincoln's drink."

Hux rocks back on his heels. "Trust me. I know who did it. Lincoln's ex spent the last decade badmouthing him around town. It was no secret there was no love loss there."

Macy shakes her head. "She moved on and remarried. Besides, why would she kill him while her current husband was having it out with the guy?"

Huxley tweaks his brows. "She's not that bright."

Jasper shakes his head. "I don't know. Whoever committed the crime knew there would be a lot of witnesses—and a lot of potential suspects. I think maybe whoever did this is smarter than we're giving them credit for."

Trixie comes to mind. I'm determined to find out exactly how smart she can be. I know for a fact she's a businesswoman—in the business of keeping herself comfortable with someone else's money.

Emmie comes over with Jamison, and soon Huxley is quickly absorbed into a conversation with them.

Jasper leans in. "Follow me," he whispers as he leads us to the corner of the room and we're joined with Leo.

I look from one to the other. “What’s going on? What did those men want?”

Jasper leans in, his expression stone-cold. “Bizzy, those men are from the MRD, an offshoot of the FBI.”

“What? Why would the FBI be at the inn? Does this have anything to do with the rash of homicides in Cider Cove?” ***Leo?*** I glance his way. ***Why do I get the feeling I’m not going to like where this is headed?***

Leo gives a slow blink. ***You won’t.***

Jasper takes my hand. “I asked that specifically and they skirted the issue.”

“What’s the MRD?” My heart thumps wildly just saying those letters out loud. “What does the acronym stand for?”

“It’s the Metaphysical Research Department.” Jasper’s chest expands. “They deal with things that may not be natural to this world.”

“Like ghosts.” I close my eyes a moment. “Or people with supernatural powers.”

“Exactly.” Jasper gives my hand a squeeze. “And I have no clue why they’re looking at the inn, other than to create some sort of sensational story out of the killings that have taken place over the last few months. Leo shut them down.”

Leo offers a short-lived smile. “That I did.” ***But mark my words. They will be back. And the kicker? They asked for you by name.***

My heart stops cold.

“Lovely,” I say as Camila catches my eye from across the room and gifts me a dark smile.

How did you like my treat, Bizzy? A laugh pumps through her as she tosses her hair back. ***I bet you and Leo would love to be alone so you could talk in private. Come to think of it, the two of you make a mighty fine couple. What do you say, Bizzy? Have I finally convinced you to give Jasper the heave-ho? Or do you need another shove in the right direction?***

I look to Leo and offer a sickly smile before meeting up with Jasper’s eyes and my heart breaks.

“Hey”—he pulls me in just as Leo heads over to Mack—“we’ll get through this together. I promise everything is going to be okay.”

I’m not so sure we’ll get through this together.

And I’m positive not a thing will be okay—not as long as Camila Ryder is in our lives or the Metaphysical Research Department.

12

Metaphysical Research Department.

I gnawed on that little horrifying tidbit all through dinner. It took everything in me not to lunge across the table and strangle Camila Report-You-to-the-Feds Ryder. Once dinner was through, I said goodbye to everyone as Georgie and I prepared to leave. Jasper walks us out front and warms me with an embrace as the icy December air slices right through my heavy winter coat.

"Drive safely," he whispers while dotting my cheek with a kiss. "And don't worry about those men. I'll do a little digging and see what that was about."

"No." It comes out a little too loud and caustic. "I mean, don't bother. You mentioned they wouldn't be back. That's good enough for me." And hopefully, everything that just spewed out of me is good enough for Jasper. But my voice shook with every word, and I don't even believe the things that flew out of my mouth.

His chest expands with his next breath. ***Knew it. She's worried. And she doesn't want me to worry. I'll get to the bottom of it for her. I won't bring it up again. No need for her to lose sleep over it.***

He pulls me close. "All right. I'll see you back at the inn." He lands a lingering kiss to my lips. "Goodnight, Georgie." He gives a friendly wave before taking off into the night.

Georgie inches my way. "Ooh, that looked steamy! I bet he'll sneak into your cottage later and give you a real kiss goodnight."

"Not if he wants to live. Having someone breaking into my cottage while I'm asleep isn't one of my go-to fantasies."

"It is mine."

I'm about to reply to that disconcerting comment when Mackenzie steps out of the restaurant.

She grunts as soon as she lays eyes on me and huffs her way over. "She's cornering Leo again. I don't know if she's more interested in my man or yours, but that beast needs to go. We need to figure out a way to get rid of her, *yesterday*. I want her gone. If only there was something we could blackmail her with."

"*Ooh*!" Georgie wiggles her fingers and squints with delight. "Now we're getting to the nitty gritty. What have you got on her, Bizzy? And by the way, who is *she*?"

"Trust me. You don't want to know." A thought comes to me.

A few weeks back, while I was investigating Camila as a suspect in another homicide, I discovered she took racy pictures for some greasy magazine called *Gear Head*. Camila played the part of a scantily clad schoolgirl—a play on the fact she's a high school counselor—while bending over a desk. She said she had just finished up a modeling shoot for a women's clothing catalog when the photographer suggested they do a few fun shots. It turns out, those fun shots made their way onto a calendar and the pictures for the women's catalog seemingly disappeared. I really did feel terrible for her. She's not proud of it and she doesn't want the word getting out. The calendar, however, is set to release next month.

I take a deep breath. "Actually, I do have something on her, but it's so terrible, if it ever comes out, she could get fired from her position at the school where she works. Although, it's probably not much of a threat at this point.

Something like this is bound to blow up sooner or later. Camila is destined to lose her job."

"Ooh!" Georgie claps her hands. "It's Camila I-Want-All-My-Exes-Back Ryder."

Mackenzie nods her way. "You got that right." She reverts those dark eyes my way. "What is it, Bizzy? What do you have on her? I'll make sure it blows up *sooner* than later."

"No. We can't cause her to lose her job. I don't want that hanging over my head."

Georgie gives a slow nod. "Bad juju."

Mackenzie smirks. "I don't believe in juju. But have it your way. I'll make the threat myself."

"She'll know I told you."

"She won't," Mack insists. "You said this would blow up. That means it's inevitable. And if it's inevitable, that means you're not the only one privy to this, Bizzy Baker. In fact, I'm betting a little internet digging will lead me right where I need to be."

Mack gasps with delight. "Don't you worry, Bizzy. Camila Ryder is already in the rearview mirror. Nobody messes with me." She wrinkles her nose over at me. "With us. See you at the cookie exchange tomorrow." Mack ducks back into the restaurant before I can protest. Hopefully, she won't find a thing.

Just as Georgie and I are about to head off to the parking lot, I glance across the street and it feels as if the heavens burst open and an entire angelic choir is about to sing the killer's name.

I link arms with Georgie as we make a mad dash in that direction.

"Where are we going?" she hollers up above the rush of wind.

"To the City Limits Bar and Grill," I shout back. "I think I need a drink." And to have a few words with Trixie Jolly-Golightly.

Inside, the City Limits Bar and Grill holds the scent of oily French fries and overpriced beer.

It's nearly pitch dark in here, save for the candles dotting the tables in the expansive room to our left. To the right there's a sign that reads *this way to the bar* and that's exactly where I drag Georgie.

Georgie gives a maniacal laugh. "This night just gets better and better. Who knew hanging out with you would be such a hoot? Blackmail, deceit, and knocking back shots at the bar. I'll have to tell Macy we were wrong. You're not uptight and high-strung. You're a pretty cool chick after all."

"Nice to know you and Macy think so highly of me." I crane my neck, trying to see past the tangle of bodies up front, and sure enough I spot a long blonde ponytail and head that way. "This is a suspect, Georgie. So just play along," I whisper.

"Oh, I'm playing this homicidal fiddle until the killer comes home, Bizzy. Do I get to say *book 'em*?"

"Not quite yet." I grimace over at her just as we hit the long, expansive bar with a cushioned vinyl wraparound. I suppose in the event one of their patrons passes out, they won't crack their head open.

Trixie Jolly-Golightly is seated at the end, and there are a slew of barstools free to her right. A barrel-chested man heads her way, and I race him to the seat next to her and make wild eyes at him until he holds up his hands and walks in the opposite direction.

I land in the seat next to Trixie, and Georgie sits by my side—hopefully, a safe distance away from the suspect at hand, but with Georgie it might still be far too close. Heck, having her back in Cider Cove might be far too close.

I look over at Trixie, but she's not paying me any mind. She's too busy hovering over a glass of brown liquor.

"*Men,*" I huff in a rather lame attempt to garner her attention.

Her shoulders slump just a little bit more as she takes a sip of her drink.

The bartender heads our way, an older gentleman with a greasy handlebar mustache, and I'm starting to wonder if this is one of those theme restaurants.

"What's it going to be, ladies?" His voice is gruff, yet friendly.

Georgie leans over the bar. "Hey, hot stuff. What's the special?"

"The special?" I practically mouth her way.

He gives a husky laugh in Georgie's direction. "Hey, hot stuff yourself. Special tonight is hot buttered rum punch."

Georgie belts out a moan that sounds as if she's lost in ecstasy.

Good grief, woman. I'm tempted to smack her. *Rein it in.*

"We'll take two." I lean in and whisper, "Make mine a virgin. I'm driving."

Georgie lifts a finger as he starts to take off. "I'm no virgin. I can prove it to you, if you like." She gives a heavy wink his way, and it takes a lot of self-control for me not to chuckle or vomit. Not only is Georgie one of my favorite people, I think of her like my grandmother—my rather virginal grandmother.

I look over at Trixie and do an exaggerated double take in her direction.

"Hey! I think I recognize you." Okay, so my acting chops could use a little polishing, but I'm not in this for an Oscar. A guilty verdict will do nicely.

The older blonde perks right up. Her affect brightens as she looks right at me. She's pretty in a made up doll sort of way. With those long, exaggerated lashes and those hot pink lips, there's a bit of a cartoonish appeal about her.

She leans in. "Did you see *Jane and Tarzan's Big Adventure in LaLa Land*?"

"Excuse me?" I inch back, trying to digest the idea. "Oh, um, no, actually. What is that?"

She waves me off, her affect falling once again. "A movie I did in my twenties. Don't worry, honey. You weren't the only one who missed it." She takes another sip of the brown sludge in front of her. "Were you a waitress at Teasers Gentlemen's Club?"

Georgie gasps, "Were you, Bizzy? Were you?"

I shoot my older counterpart a look, but before I can instill an iota of fear in Georgie, the friendly bartender is back with our drinks and flirting heavily with her.

"No," I say to Trixie. "I wasn't a waitress there. I actually remember you from the other night on Candy Cane Lane. I was walking with my boyfriend and we came upon that horrible scene. How are you doing?"

Her expression sours in an instant. "Oh, that." She pushes her drink away. "Lincoln Brooks was *my* boyfriend. And he's dead and gone like yesterday's news. That's what happens when you get old. You die." ***Only he wasn't all that old—and I doubt it was his time to die.***

"So he died of natural causes?" I shake my head because I can't maintain the disbelief. Unless, of course, she doesn't know the truth, and that might be the case.

"It depends. Would you call death by antifreeze and oleander natural?"

"What?" It squawks out of me so loud I sound like a chicken with the threat of having its feathers plucked out. I knew about the antifreeze, but oleander? "Is that what the sheriff's department said?"

She hikes a brow. "It's what I said. Trust me. I have it on good authority."

"Oleander, huh?" No sooner do I get the words out than Georgie slaps her hand down in front of me.

"I knew it!" Georgie leans in hard. "It's those bushes in front of that creepy Santa's place across the street. I bet they did it, Bizzy. It's always the ex-wife. Song as old as time. It's clear this woman is innocent."

"Kill me." I close my eyes an inordinate amount of time. Note to self: Never bring Georgie along while investigating a suspect again.

Trixie slaps the bar in front of me as well. "I think the old beady-eyed witch did it, too!" Her own eyes are wild with delight and I try to pry into her mind, but it's gone to static. She's either deliberately hiding something or she's genuinely excited at the thought of nailing Mary Beth to a homicide. "I told Lincoln for years he had better watch his back." She takes a moment to point my way. "Nothing good comes from living across the street from your ex. You can quote me on that."

Georgie shakes her head. "Bizzy isn't a reporter. She's an innkeeper. She works down at the Country Cottage Inn at the edge of Cider Cove. You should come visit sometime."

Perfect. And if Trixie is the killer, she'll know exactly where to deliver a special drink mixed just for me.

Trixie nods over at Georgie as if she appreciated the invitation. "I might just do that. You've got that cute little café and that white powder beach right outside the facility. I've been there a few times. Lincoln used to take me. He always took me to nice places. I already miss that." ***And***

not much else, but I'll keep the commentary to myself.

"I'm sorry for your loss," I say.

She flicks her wrist. "Don't be. We weren't getting along toward the end anyhow. I mean, don't get me wrong. He could be a sweet prince when he wanted to be. But, most of the time he played the part of the wicked king."

"Don't they all," Georgie groans. "Preach it, sister."

Trixie leans over and gives her a high five, and suddenly I feel like a third wheel while they bond over booze and bad boyfriends.

"So the ex-wife"—I start—"is that who you think did it?"

Trixie gives a slow, rather convincing nod. "Oh, hon, I've seen them war it out over a misplaced box of tissues. They could summon World War Three over just about anything. And that new husband of hers was a beaut. Sometimes I'd wonder who was more obsessed with Lincoln, Mary Beth or Dexter."

"What do they do for a living?" I ask. "Do you know?"

The bartender slides another drink Trixie's way and she happily accepts it.

Her hot pink lips twitch. "She's a busybody. PTA, HOA—you know the type. They live to make you crazy. But

I don't think she leaves that house to punch a time card. And he owns Bronson's Auto Shop out in Edison."

"Oh my goodness!" Georgie belts it out as if she just took a bullet. "I bet that's where the antifreeze came from! I bet they tag-teamed him. The wife crushed the oleander leaves and the husband doused it with antifreeze."

Trixie gives a wild nod. "Now you're onto something!"

"No, no," I say as I sag into my seat. "Everyone in these parts has antifreeze lying around in the garage." I think on it a moment. "And I'm not entirely sure how rare the oleander bushes are."

Georgie snorts. "Are you kidding? They're like weeds. I've got 'em on the side of my cottage. Any fool could get their hands on that stuff."

Trixie lifts a brow. "But any fool didn't. It was Mary Beth, and I can prove it."

"*How*?" both Georgie and I sing in unison.

How this went from an earnest undercover operation to a bumbling musical, I will never know. But I'm betting the delicious hot buttered rum has something to do with it.

Trixie's chest bucks with a silent laugh. "Good old Mary Beth was having an affair with Lincoln right up until his untimely death."

My mouth falls open. "How can you be sure?"

She fishes the cherry out of her drink and plucks it off into her mouth. “I caught them in the act.”

“No!” Georgie wails and Trixie is quick to nod her way.

“Yup. In fact, that’s the reason I wouldn’t say yes when he proposed.”

Georgie scoffs. “He proposed?”

Trixie sighs. “He sure did. Got down on one brand new knee and everything. But he just wouldn’t quit messing with his ex. I knew about it for the last solid year. Apparently, they’ve been having a feast of the flesh ever since they parted matrimonial ways. Poor Dexter didn’t know about it. I asked Lincoln to knock it off. He wanted me to quit my side gig of playing the part of arm candy for well-to-do men, but he refused to keep Mary Beth out of his bedroom.” A hearty growl comes from her. “The nerve.”

“Trixie.” I shake my head just enough. “You said you knew about the affair for a year. Why on earth would you stay with him?”

She flashes her red glittery fingernails my way. “I’m what they call high-maintenance. This work of art isn’t going to pay for itself. Lincoln had needs, and I had wants. It was a give-and-take relationship that worked out just fine for us. I think he just wanted to marry me so he could stop making his monthly payment.” She bumps her shoulder to mine. “My time isn’t cheap, honey, and yours shouldn’t be either.”

The thought of charging Jasper cold hard cash to spend time with me makes me cringe.

Georgie snaps her fingers. “Maybe the ex-wife didn’t do it. Maybe Dexter found out about the affair, and that’s why he was in such a rage that night. A man in a Santa suit doesn’t get riled up over nothing.”

Trixie moans at the thought as she shakes her head. “I don’t know. Dex was pretty angry. I mean, he just raced across the street like a bullet and went straight for Lincoln. But it was Mary Beth who was dealing with the refreshments.” ***So was I, but I’m keeping that tidbit to myself. The last thing I need is the Seaview Sheriff’s Department knocking down my door. The man is dead. I don’t want to think about him or what he cost me.***

I swallow hard. “Have you made peace—you know, with his passing?”

She takes a breath. “No, but I will soon enough.” ***In exactly twenty-four hours when that will of his is unleashed. I’m in it, and I can’t wait to get my hands on what’s mine.*** She lifts her drink. “To Lincoln Brooks. May he rest in peace.” ***And may I get every last piece of his fortune he left behind.***

We button up our visit with Trixie, and I let her know all about the Let It Snow charity event at the Country Cottage Inn on Saturday night. I even go as far as letting her know she can have a free ticket.

"Charity event?" She fans herself with her glittering nails. "Why, an event like that is liable to bring out all sorts of wealthy men. Count me in, honey. I'll be there with my jingle bells on."

"Perfect," I tell her. "We'll see you then."

Georgie and I set out to leave but not before Georgie gets the bartender's number.

"She shoots, she scores!" Georgie wags her phone at me as we make our way through the bitter cold night to the parking lot across the street.

"I scored, too," I say as we hop into my car and head toward Cider Cove.

All the way home I think about Mary Beth Bronson and those oleander bushes.

13

If there's one thing that I look forward to as the manager of the Country Cottage Inn, it's the fact each year the inn plays host to the official Cider Cove cookie exchange.

The scent of cookies in every one of its delicious configurations lights up the air, and it's a sugary delight to all of my senses.

All of my life I've had an intense yearning to bake. Just the thought of mixing, measuring, sifting, pouring delicious batter into pans, and baking a sweet treat has thrilled me. And, truth be told, that's about as far as I can get in the endeavor before everything goes south. I either undercook, overcook, or char to an unrecognizable crisp everything I dare put in the oven. Thankfully, Emmie has shared my yearning to bake and was lucky enough to carry out the endeavor with the expert ease of a Parisian pastry chef. Eventually, I accepted my lot in the kitchen and have worked with Emmie on perfecting recipes that she could bring to life in a way that the human palate can more than appreciate them. Like, for example, the gingerbread whoopie pies. After hours of tweaking the recipe, we finally agreed on the finished product. Which, if I do say so myself, is absolute glorious perfection.

And that brings me right back to the cookie exchange. The inn is bustling with women as they hurry and shuttle in their delectable desserts to the inn's formal dining room, where we have tables laden with every baked good under the rarely seen winter sun. Cheery Christmas carols belt from the speakers as the sound of happy chattering and intermittent bursts of laughter fill the air. Just about everyone here has donned a Christmas sweater with an emblem of the season represented over the front. But this is no ugly sweater party. This is the real deal. And each sweater is worn with pride. Most of these sweaters are classic treasures that are resurrected each Christmas season to be worn to a special event much like this one. And each year I get a kick out of seeing how many sweaters I can remember from the year before.

Emmie and the rest of the kitchen staff worked overtime to make sure we had more than enough gingerbread whoopie pies to participate in today's festivities. And both my mother and Georgie baked up a storm of their own and brought their offerings to the dessert table. The exchange is well underway as women walk around filling platters with a mix of every sweet treat laid out before them, so I step back out to the front counter to help direct the foot traffic of those still streaming inside.

The inn looks resplendent with Christmas trees strewn with white twinkle lights in every room. There's one in the entry just past the foyer that stands twelve feet tall and is festooned with giant cherry red bows. An animatronic angel sits on top whose wings move smoothly in and out. Each feathered wing is covered in fiber optic lights that give it an enchanted like appeal. Just this morning, Jordy set out the nativity scene at the base of the tree and guests haven't stopped taking pictures of it. The rest of the inn is covered with garland and twinkle lights everywhere you look, and even the long marble counter is dotted with red poinsettias.

I find Fish hiding out behind my chair, while Mistletoe and Holly enjoy all the attention they want as they sit on a red and green crochet runner that Nessa laid out for them on the counter. Nothing brings out the best in people like two tiny little kittens who love to be held.

A tall, dark, and vexingly handsome homicide detective strides on in with Sherlock Bones by his side, looking like he finally has his spring back in his step. Now that the cone of shame has been taken off for good, he's almost forgiven us. *Almost.*

"I see Sherlock's right back to his old self again," I say, giving the happy-go-lucky pooch a scratch between the ears.

I am, Bizzy. Can I play with Fish? I miss biting her in half and I have an awful craving for kitten.

I wince at the thought.

"Be careful with Fish," I say to the excited pup. "Her stitches have just healed. I'm afraid you can't put her in your mouth just yet."

Sherlock groans with defeat as he makes his way to her.

"Detective." I bite down on a flirtatious smile before I remember the details of my meeting with Trixie last night and that smile melts right off. I step around the counter and land a quick kiss to his lips. "Guess what?"

His head inches back, and I'd swear there's a slight frown on his face.

"You've got good news for me?" ***After that research I did, I'm not sure what kind of news I have for her.***

My lips part a moment. "Yes, I've got good news. I think I know who killed Lincoln Brooks."

"What?" He takes me by the hand and leads me over to the tree as his spiced cologne intoxicates me. "I'm all ears."

"I think Mary Beth did it. I found out she was having an affair with Lincoln this entire time, and I bet he threatened to rat her out. I think she took antifreeze from either her garage or her husband's shop and mixed it with the oleander bushes she has in the front of her house and she poisoned him in order to keep their secret from getting out."

"Bizzy"—the muscles in his jaw tense and he looks unfairly handsome—"how did you know the plant toxin that was mixed with the antifreeze was oleander?"

My mouth opens and closes like a marionette's. "Okay." I blow out a breath. "I met with Trixie Jolly-Golightly at a bar across the street from Maximus last night."

"What?" He squeezes his eyes shut tight. "Why would you meet up with a suspect in a homicide investigation at a bar? Were you waiting for me to leave?"

"What? No!" I wince. "But when you did leave is when I noticed the sign—and I was told that's the very bar she likes to languish in, so I practically felt obligated to go. It was like fate or kismet."

"Or a potential disaster." His brows hitch. "Bizzy, you endangered yourself."

"Georgie was with me," I say as if that makes everything better. "And besides, she scored the bartender's number." I give a little shrug.

He takes a moment to digest this information. "Bizzy, I just got the official report from toxicology yesterday. Nobody knows it was oleander in that cup other than the coroner and me."

I suck in a quick breath. "How did Trixie know?"

His cheek rides up one side. "Because she's probably the killer."

I clap my hand over my mouth. "But she gave such a convincing argument that Mary Beth was the killer. And she was believable, Jasper. I swear you would have believed her, too."

"I have no doubt. But I would have also known she's a con woman. Her real name is Wilhelmina Fletcher, and she's been conning men out of their pensions and nest eggs for years."

"I know that." I wrinkle my nose. " Okay, so I didn't know her real name, but she all but admitted that she was a paid escort. Why do you think she would kill him?" Those thoughts she had about the will come to mind and I moan. "She's in his will."

"I would think so. And that might just be the motivator. Anyway, I guess I'd better track her down and see if I can get her to tell me how she knew about the oleander. It looks like I'll have to take her in for questioning."

I glance to the entry just as Leo Granger walks in, clad in his sheriff's deputy uniform, and heads this way.

"Leo." Jasper wipes down his face. "Glad you could make it." He looks back my way. "I asked Leo to come down. I wanted to share what I gleaned regarding the Metaphysical Research Department. It turns out, the agency is based in Nevada, somewhere near Groom Lake."

Leo leans in. "Groom Lake? That's next to Area 51."

"Area 51?" I balk. "As in the fabled place that deals with aliens?" ***Oh, Leo, we are in bigger trouble than we know.***

His brows depress, but he doesn't let a single thought fly—most likely because he agrees with me.

Jasper takes a breath. "The MRD is one of many offshoots of the FBI. They typically make their way to the

McCarran Airport in Las Vegas and enter a private terminal where they board unmarked planes known by the acronym JANET—Joint Air Network Transpiration. Only those with top security clearance are allowed to work with the MRD. This organization is no joke. And they wouldn't come all the way to Cider Cove, Maine unless they felt a very real need. To say they went out of their way is an understatement."

Leo and I exchange a brief glance.

Leo shakes his head. "Don't worry. They're probably scoping out the inn as a possible base for their employees while they're out doing whatever it is they do. It's nice, and out of the way. I bet the things they're dealing with are nowhere near Cider Cove."

"I sure hope so." I give a single nod his way. ***Nice save.***

Jasper pulls out his phone and glances at the time. "I'd better get going." He looks to Leo. "There's been a break in the Brooks' murder. Bizzy here picked up a hard lead, and I need to check it out before the killer figures out they sold the farm." He lands a kiss to my cheek before hitching his head to the door. "Leo, you're coming with me."

"In case you need backup?" Leo asks with a touch of amusement in his tone.

To keep you the heck away from Bizzy. He gives a short-lived smile. ***The guy can't stop looking at her. Not that I blame him. And not that I trust his motives. The last thing I want is to put Bizzy in that position.***

"Yes, for backup," Jasper concedes. ***Whatever it takes.***

I watch as Jasper and Leo leave before I take off for the dining hall and begin nibbling on the first sweet treat I see, one of my mother's raspberry jelly thumbprint cookies, a tried-and-true favorite at our house growing up.

Mackenzie spots me and excuses herself from the small crowd she's entertaining to head my way.

"Mayor Woods." I give an amicable nod. "That public nuisance we discussed is at it again." I pull a tight smile. There is no way I'm telling Mack the truth about what Camila knows—heaven forbid Camila tells *her*. Not that anything that comes out of Camila's mouth is credible at the moment. Her desperation has clouded her judgment and by proxy turned her into someone with questionable morals. Everyone knows lying is just a stone's throw from stealing someone else's boyfriend. "When are you going to act?"

Mackenzie tips her head back and laughs. “I already have the ball in motion. Expect results sooner than you think.”

Camila and Gwyneth step into the room and Mack glowers in their direction before taking in a sharp breath and flexing that contrived smile she’s honed so well since she’s taken office.

“I’ll do what I can, with what I have, Bizzy. Enjoy the afternoon.” Mack takes off, and I think back to that conversation I had with Jasper and Leo. Camila has no idea the destruction she’s about to rain down on my life. Not that she cares. As long as I’m out of Jasper’s life, it won’t matter to her if I’m here at the inn or in some fabled part of Nevada. Camila is only looking out for her own selfish interests. Namely the one I’m interested in—Jasper.

Speaking of Jasper, he’s off to question Trixie, or Wilhelmina for that matter. A part of me can’t believe she killed Lincoln.

And what about that stuff she said about Mary Beth? Would Mary Beth really have an affair with her ex right under her husband’s nose? And if Dexter knew about it would he have killed Lincoln? It’s not a leap to think he’s capable. I saw hatred in his eyes that night he was arguing with Lincoln. I’d love to have a chance to talk to Dexter and hear what he has to say—or more to the point, hear what he's thinking.

Emmie comes my way and slings an arm around my shoulder as we watch the women chattering and laughing around us.

"Well, Bizzy, it looks as if we have another successful cookie exchange under our belts. What do you want to do now?"

I press my lips tight a moment. "I think I want to drive down to Edison and have my car inspected. You up for riding shotgun?"

Her lids hood a notch because, face it, Emmie Crosby has always had the ability to see right through me.

"We're questioning a suspect, aren't we?"

I tip my head to the side and nod.

"Great." She claps her hands together as if she were greedy to do just that. "Let's grab some cookies for the road. I'll take the left side of the room. You take the right."

We do just that, and we munch all the way to a tiny little auto shop in downtown Edison.

Dexter Bronson, I hope you're ready to spill everything you know. I'm getting the truth out of you today. Even if I have to bribe you with a cookie or two.

14

"They say a way to a man's heart is through his stomach. Let's hope the way to his confession is along the same route," I say to Emmie as we pull into Bronson's Auto Shop.

Emmie squints out the window. "I'm pretty sure those cookies are bound to work a miracle here. This place looks like it's home to desolation and despair."

It's true. In a technicolor world, this tiny speck on Edison's map looks like a sepia tone dumpster from an era long gone by. Cars sit eroding and seemingly abandoned on the side of the property, and there's a small line of newer make and models with their hoods and trunks popped open while a small beehive of men buzz around them.

I spot Dexter over by the open garage looking over some paperwork attached to a clipboard. And just behind him there's a faded Christmas wreath hung over the door to the facility that looks as if it's seen better seasons gone by.

"How about we divide and conquer?" I hand Emmie the larger platter of the two. "I'll corner Dexter on his own. You make sure the rest of the men have all they want to eat. We'll let them know we're sharing the overflow from the cookie exchange."

Emmie grunts out a laugh. "Oh, Bizzy, they're men. They'll see a plate full of cookies and their minds will turn to fuzz right after. They won't come looking for an explanation."

"Hopefully, Dexter's mind won't turn to fuzz."

We get out, and without having to draw much attention to our offerings, men come out of the woodwork and congregate around Emmie and her cookie platter while I make a beeline for Dexter.

"Hello!" I say it as cheery as can be. The air is so icy it feels as if my lungs will freeze with every breath I take. It snowed last night, just enough to cover the ground, and since Edison is west of Cider Cove, it is certainly sticking.

Dexter looks up and his lips curve into a smile. "How can I help you?"

"We're just delivering cookies to any and every business that will take them. We had a local cookie exchange that was a little too productive." I hold out the platter to him, brimming with holiday treats of every shape and size.

"Say no more." He picks up a gingerbread whoopie pie without hesitation and takes a bite. "Mmm, now that's what I call heaven. You could sell these and make a fortune. In fact, my kids are dabbling in that business right now. We've got a cookie stand on the corner at night that caters to the crowds coming through the area. I live over in what's known as Candy Cane Lane, a place out in Cider Cove."

"Oh, I'm from Cider Cove, too. Speaking of which, I was just at Candy Cane Lane about a week ago. Hey?" I turn up the volume on my smile. "Did we meet?" I wince. "I'm sorry. My mother introduced me to so many people that horrible night. The kids in my neighborhood are calling it the night Santa died. I was actually in front of that poor man's house when he keeled over. It was such a horrible scene."

He tips his head back. "I was there, too. And we might have met. But I meet hundreds of people each night, so it's hard for me to keep them all straight. No offense."

"No offense taken. So you saw it, too?"

"The dead guy? Oh, yeah. I was the other Santa on the lawn with him. Lincoln and I didn't always get along. Come to think of it, I don't know who he actually got along with.

No kids. Lots of money. That will send the vultures circling, I'm sure."

"Can I ask why he was so hard to get along with?"

He takes another bite out of his whoopie pie. "I don't know. A part of me thinks that Lincoln actually liked having enemies."

"I heard a rumor that he liked the ladies a little too much." I shrug over at him, hoping to prod some sort of admission from him.

"Yes." His gaze hardens on something across the street. "He liked the ladies a little too much." ***He seemed to like my wife a heck of a lot. I should have killed him the second I found out about the two of them together. What on earth Mary Beth saw in him is beyond me.***

It's true! Mary Beth and Lincoln *were* having an affair. And what does Dexter mean by he should have killed him the second he found out? As in, he waited until that night? Or someone beat him to it?

"What do you think happened?" I ask as he finishes up his dessert and hold the tray out for him to take another.

"I think one of those women decided she didn't like him so much after all." He takes up a confetti sprinkled sugar cookie. "They poisoned him. He died a horrible death right there in front of all those kids. That was selfish of the killer. I get they wanted him dead, but what about all the Christmas magic people like us work hard to maintain for the next generation? Any other time of year would have been better."

"I agree. But why would he have all those women up in arms? Do you really think they'd be mad enough to kill?"

"I sure do." He gives a wistful shake of the head. ***I was certainly mad enough to do it.*** "I heard his girlfriend was a suspect." His lips purse. ***And my wife.*** "Trixie something or other. I knew she was trouble the moment I met her. She's a kept woman, only Lincoln couldn't quite figure out how to keep her. Some women—kept or not—don't really want to be tied down." ***Mary Beth for instance.*** He glowers past me.

"I heard he was having an affair with someone, and that his girlfriend got wind of it."

His eyes widen a notch and a fire flashes through them. I've clearly overstepped my bounds.

"I heard the same thing." ***I saw the way he and Mary Beth went on. I knew she was visiting him. Mary Beth should have known better. Heck, Lincoln should have known better. But there's nothing sweeter than revenge and, I guess now that Lincoln is dead, I've got my revenge on them both.***

On them both?

My stomach cinches.

My goodness, could Dexter here have framed his wife for the murder?

He takes a breath as that smile returns to his face.

"Julia was the other woman." He shrugs. "His secretary. She's his side piece." ***I'm leaving Mary Beth out of it. But then, bringing up Julia isn't most likely stretching the truth. The guy bagged everything that moved.*** "I saw them getting friendly in front of his house one day. I asked him about it and he said he liked them young. His poor girlfriend was either clueless or looked the other way. I'm guessing it was the latter. She was stepping out on him as well. It was a horrible, twisted situation." ***And you don't know the half of it.*** "But it's over." ***And I'm hoping by the new year, this entire nightmare goes away.*** "Now if those bumbling detectives can find the killer by Christmas, we can all sleep a little easier."

"But it was personal, right?" I lift a shoulder. "I mean, if we cling to that, we can all sleep soundly as it is."

"Suit yourself. I just don't like the fact someone out there feels as if they got away with it." ***Getting away with murder. Now there's a feather for the old hat.***

I hold my breath a second, hoping for one more piece of incriminating evidence. Not that he hasn't already given me plenty.

"Thank you for the treats." He points down at another gingerbread whoopie pie and I nod as he takes it. "Never tasted anything so good in my life. It's like the whole Christmas season is encapsulated in a cookie."

"I agree. Have a good rest of the day," I give a little wave as he heads into the garage and I see an odd sign that catches my attention.

Season's best antifreeze half off! Proprietary blend sold only at this location! Works twice as hard as most top brands.

I pull out my phone and take a picture of the signage.

Lincoln was poisoned with antifreeze. I wonder if we can narrow down what type? I wonder what it would mean if it was from Dexter's shop?

The murderous possibilities are endless.

15

Later that night, I head over to Candy Cane Lane where the streets and sidewalks alike are once again bustling with people bundled in their winter coats, with scarves wrapped all the way up to their noses.

It's literally elbow-to-elbow out there and parking is scarce. I had to park in the neighborhood up above and hike down a steep incline just to get to the cheery holiday scene, which feels a lot more chaotic than it ever does peaceful tonight. Not to mention the inclement weather. The wind is howling, and it's tipping over those large cheery holiday blowups everyone seems to have fastened to their lawns. The lights festooned on just about every house swing wild in the wind, and there are hats being blown right off of people's heads and scarves that fly like kites.

Christmas Eve is just two days away. It doesn't help that it's Friday night and every organization known to man has shuttled out buses and buses of children to see what Candy Cane Lane has to offer. It's just Sherlock Bones and me tonight. When Mistletoe and Holly found out where I was headed, they begged me not to take them. I think they're still fearing I'll give them back to Mary Beth.

During our last visit, Georgie had them sit on Dexter's lap while he was dressed as Santa and Mary Beth tried to pet them, and let's just say all clawing and pawing heck broke loose. So, of course, Fish offered to stay home with them.

Jasper is working late tonight. Georgie has a hot date with that bartender we met at the City Limits Bar and Grill. The one serving up the hot buttered *buns*—her words, not mine. And anyway, I highly advised her to stay away from anything hot and buttered for the night.

Earlier, I asked Macy to meet me out here and she still hasn't responded.

My phone pings and I walk Sherlock to the side to avoid being run over by the onslaught of strollers and roving packs of teenagers.

It's a text from Macy. **Why would I want to walk around in subzero weather, looking at a bunch of lights, when I could be snug in my bed watching**

mysteries and ordering up a whole new wardrobe online?

"Point taken." I shake my head at the screen before shoving the phone into my purse. "It looks like it's just you and me, Sherlock. You ready to do this?"

He gives a howling bark. ***I'm ready, Bizzy. I want to see Santa again. He had a biscuit for me and everything. And there's a poodle that lives two doors away from him who said it would be okay if I sniff her—***

"Okay!" I say bright and cheery with just a touch of olfactory horror. "No sniffing."

My nose twitches as we resume our walk in the thicket of people all bundled for a night out in the elements. A few of the neighbors have bonfires right there in their driveways in cute round outdoor fireplaces, and there are lines ten deep at the cookie stand manned by the Bronsons' children. We get as far as the corner before one of the street vendors selling glowing red antlers plops an illuminated headband over Sherlock's head, and the crowd around us coos at the adorable sight.

Bizzy? Sherlock gives me a wild look, and I bite down on a smile. ***I look ridiculous, don't I?***

"You look amazing."

"Ten bucks," the young man selling them shouts my way. "But we'll make it five for the dog. They look good on him."

I dig out a five-dollar bill and hand it over before Sherlock and I cross the street with a sea of people.

Bizzy, why is everyone staring and taking pictures of me?

A small laugh bounces through me. It's true. Hordes of teenagers and mothers with small children all have their phones positioned in his direction.

"Sherlock, you're the cutest reindeer that ever did live," I say as we navigate our way through a human wave like a couple of salmon swimming upstream until we come upon a couple of familiar faces.

My stomach sours, but only because it's a natural effect that Mackenzie has had on me ever since she shoved me into that whiskey barrel way back when.

"Mayor Woods." I offer an amicable nod. "Leo."

"Bizzy Baker." Mack sheds her signature chiding grin. She looks stunning tonight with her fitted emerald green coat and her dark hair swarming around her shoulders in smooth creamy waves. Mack has always had the ability to look impeccable despite things that disrupt the lives of mere mortals, such as hurricane strength winds.

It's almost eerie the way she doesn't have a hair out of place.

"Bizzy." Leo nods my way as he gives a quick pat to Sherlock. He's dressed in his own clothes tonight, not a single stitch that screams Seaview Sheriff's Department. "You're quite the lady killer tonight, Sherlock. The antlers are a good look on you."

Mackenzie takes a moment to glower at the sweet pooch, "What brings you here tonight, Bizzy?"

I glance to Leo. "The same thing that brings everyone else here. I'm just trying to soak in the season. It has a way of disappearing before you know it."

Mack's phone pings in her hand, and she groans as she looks to the screen. "I need to get down the street. The city council has come by, and it's time to say a few nice words. Wish me luck. Every house is uglier than the next." She stalks off, headlong into the blustery wind.

Leo steps in with those curious eyes hooked to mine. "What really brings you here tonight?"

I glance to the left a few houses down where dozens of kids are waiting impatiently to see Dexter in his deluxe plush Santa suit.

He glances back. "Ah, yes, Bizzy Baker, detective extraordinaire. Why do I get the feeling Jasper doesn't know about this?"

“Oh, he does.” I give an incredulous laugh. “I invited him, but he’s working late and couldn’t make it.” I’m about to tell him all about my adventure out in Edison this afternoon when something catches my eye across the street at Lincoln Brooks’ house. “Leo, look,” I whisper as I take a step closer. “The front door is wide open and so is the trunk of that car parked out front.”

“I’d better check it out.” He pats his back, checking for his weapon just the way I’ve seen Jasper do a hundred times before.

“Not without me you’re not.”

Leo and I make our way across the street. We could have made it here in half the time if so many people hadn’t stopped to take a selfie with Sherlock. I can’t say I blame them. Aside from the Santa—who happens to reek of cheap rum according to Macy’s last adventure here—Sherlock is the star of the show.

“Leo”—I butt my shoulder up against his as we see a shadow moving from inside Lincoln’s house—“do you think we should call the sheriff’s department?”

“Bizzy, I am the sheriff’s department.”

The three of us make our way up the lawn, and it just so happens the fake snow is covered with the real deal tonight as the blue glow from the twinkle lights buried underneath it give it a fairy-tale appeal. The gold throne sits askew and abandoned at the moment, and no one has bothered to fix the Christmas lights that have unhitched themselves last week. Instead, the wind blows them around like a demonic whip.

A person charges out of Lincoln's front door with an armful of clothing and shoes that dangle precariously from their grasp. It's not until she makes a beeline for the trunk of the car do I see a long blonde ponytail swinging in the wind.

"Trixie?" I shout as Sherlock and I head over ahead of Leo. "What's going on?" I ask, trying to sound friendly as she dumps the load in her arms into the trunk and squints over at me. "I was at the bar last night with you." I give a little wave.

"Oh, right." She's quick to flick her wrist my way. "Didn't I say men would always disappoint you?" She slams the trunk of her car shut, and a sleeve from a sweater is left hanging outside of it, giving it an overall morbid appeal.

"Actually, I don't remember you saying that." I wince because I'm guessing I should have just gone with it.

"Well, I meant to." She plucks the purse off her arm and tosses it into the passenger's seat. "That old coot deserved to die." She pitches her head back and spits onto the ground next to her. "He's right where he should have been all along. Six feet under with no one to care." She leans in my way. "You be good to yourself, missy."

"Oh, I will." A prickling of fear pulsates from me as she prepares to take off. I'm mostly terrified I won't get another chance to shake her down for clues. Speaking of which. "Hey, Trixie? How did you know Lincoln was poisoned with oleander?"

Her eyes connect with mine a second too long but not a single thought rides through her mind.

"Let's just say I've got boyfriends in high places—like the morgue. I asked the cops what did Lincoln in, but they weren't talking so I found someone who would. I don't appreciate being held in the dark, and my friend felt the need to enlighten me."

"Well, thank you for enlightening me," I say. "I'll still see you at the Let It Snow event tomorrow night, right? There will be lots of eligible bachelors that I'm guessing will be more than willing to make you forget about your troubles."

She snarls over at the house behind us with its gaping door and lights still on inside.

"You betcha I'll be there. I'm not losing out on a sparkling future just because I had a rotten past. No man is worth it." She shakes her fist at the sky. "Hear that, Lincoln Love-'Em-and-Leave-'Em-Broke-and-Penniless? I'll be finding me a new man in less than twenty-four hours. Take that to the grave!" She hops into her sedan and speeds off, honking her way past the crowd until she's effectively stuck in traffic a few houses down.

"Well, that was dramatic." I turn to Leo with a laugh caught in my throat just as Julia pops out from the walkway on the side of the house.

Julia chuckles. "It was rather dramatic, wasn't it?" She extends a hand to Leo. "Julia Hart. I live in the carriage house in the back. I used to be the secretary for the man who lived here."

"Nice to meet you." Leo offers a brief smile. "What was the drama all about? And were those clothes hers, or was she stealing?"

Julia's chest pumps at the thought. "Oh, who cares. It's all headed to some thrift shop next week anyway. But I'm pretty sure she cleared out her own closet. Even though she didn't technically live here, Trixie had quite the collection of designer gowns and expensive coats. I'm not too surprised she wanted to scoop up what she could. Especially after the evening she's had."

"Do you mind if I ask what happened?" I tilt my head her way because I don't want to miss a single word.

Julia pulls her dark sweater tight around her body. "Reading of the will. Let's just say it didn't exactly go her way. Lincoln had lots of money, and he left none of it to her." She takes a moment to glance across the street at the Bronsons' residence. "And it went exactly how Mary Beth planned." She shakes her head. "I knew she was sniffing around for nefarious reasons. Apparently, Lincoln left her this house. Which was unexpected since it was supposed to dissolve with the rest of his estate and pay off any outstanding debts. Boy was Calvin steamed." She twitches her nose at Leo. "Calvin was Lincoln's business partner, and he sort of got caught holding the financial bag." Her eyes shift across the street once again. "But Mary Beth won the jackpot. It really makes her look maniacal like she plotted the whole thing out. First, she slept with him and had him change his will. Next, she poisoned him, and now she collects a house worth over a million dollars." She shakes her head. "Some people get away with everything. Even murder." She sniffs the air. "It was nice meeting you, Leo. And Bizzy, it was nice knowing you. My position came through in South Carolina. I'm leaving Monday."

"Wow, Santa delivered right on time. Congratulations on the position. I'll be sad to see you go. But you're still coming to the Let It Snow event at the inn, right?"

She takes a deep breath. "I don't know. I should probably pack my things. And there are still so many things to take care of for Lincoln. All those accounts of his had to be notified, and there are still a few I need to take care of."

"Well, how about just stop by long enough for me to give you a care package of gingerbread whoopie pies and a hug?"

She belts out a laugh. "Boy, you play hardball. Fine. I'll be there. You had me at whoopie pies. Have a good night." She gives Sherlock a quick pat. "The first thing I'm going to do when I get to South Carolina is pick up a shelter dog that looks exactly like you." She takes off into the murky darkness of the walkway and disappears out of sight.

Leo raises his brows my way. "You're going to have a cast of characters at the inn tomorrow night, aren't you?"

"Camila and Mack will be there, and so will you, so I guess that's true."

"Very funny."

We amble our way across the street to our intended target, and I tell Leo all about my strange meeting with Dexter yesterday. And all about his even stranger wife.

"Geez." Leo rocks back on his heels as he inspects the Bronsons' home lit up like a Christmas version of the Las Vegas strip. "And those are the oleander bushes?" He shakes his head. "Did you pick up a bottle of the antifreeze?"

"No. But I took a picture of it." I pull out my phone and show him. Leo frowns at it as if it somehow offended him.

"Come here." He navigates us up the driveway and around the masses of people all waiting for a turn to sit on Dexter Bronson's lap. Mary Beth is dressed as a rather scary looking elf tonight with garish red lipstick and giant hot pink dots on the apples of her cheeks while handing out candy canes to the kids after they're done whispering their Christmas wish to the jolly old elf.

Leo leans my way. "The garage is open," he whispers.

A small swarm gathers around Sherlock, and soon the kids in line are all circling around him while their parents angle to take pictures of him.

I glance over at the dark cave of the garage and note a lawnmower, a few tools scattered around, and in the corner, right next to the entry sits a row of at least a dozen of those specialty bottles of antifreeze Dexter was advertising at his shop.

I suck in a quick breath. ***Leo, I see them. What should I do?***

He gives a quick glance that way as he takes the leash from me. ***Pretend to drop something from your purse and chase it. That tote bag you're carrying***

could fit a human inside. Pick up a bottle and drop it in.

That's theft. I shoot him a look.

That's creative borrowing. You can bring it back while the killer is being arraigned for murder charges. That is, if it's not used as admissible evidence.

The crowd only seems to thicken around us. I dig a tissue out of my purse—or tote bag as Leo called it— as if I were about to blow my nose, and sure enough the wind carries it right over to the garage for me. I do my best to chase after it, and it gets stuck right up against a bottle of that antifreeze. I swipe both the tissue and the antifreeze up and bury them in my purse without hesitation.

My entire body breaks out into a sweat as I hurry my way back to Leo.

"It's time to go," I pant.

Leo leads us down the driveway and down the street as if the neighborhood were on fire.

A man with a heavy coat steps right in front of me, blocking my path, and I look up to see Jasper Wilder's flashing silver eyes.

"Jasper." I wrap my arms around him for a moment and pull back as he lands a kiss to my cheek. The bright look on his face dims when he sees Leo, and he quickly takes Sherlock's leash from him. "What's going on?"

A woman steps up from behind Jasper, a laugh caught in her throat. She's dressed in black from head to toe with a face that looks as if it could launch a thousand missiles—something far more destructive than a plain old ship. After all, she did start a war when she dragged a government agency into our lives.

A jumble of words tries to escape me all at once. "We were just... Mayor Woods is speaking tonight and I bought antlers." I glance to Sherlock who is busy cowering away from Camila. He's not her biggest fan.

Why are they together, Bizzy? Sherlock moans. ***Why? It's not happening again, is it?***

I certainly hope nothing will ever happen between these two again.

A husky laugh escapes her. "Well, well. It looks as if Bizzy and Leo have something to hide." She leans up against Jasper. "And I bet it's something *big*." She gives a wink my way. "I'll see you back at the inn, Bizzy. My favorite home sweet home."

Leo quickly says goodnight and takes off, and Jasper says goodnight to Camila as he walks me to my car.

"I ran into her." He winces. "Sorry."

"Don't apologize. And I highly doubt it was coincidence she saw you here. She's a proficient stalker."

His dark brows depress as he wraps his arms around me. "How about we get back to my cottage and I make us something to eat?"

"He cooks?" I tease. "I'm intrigued."

"Don't be. It's a rather small menu I'm capable of. I hope you like grilled cheese."

"Only if there's extra cheese."

His chest bumps with a laugh. "You are my kind of girl, Bizzy Baker."

I glance over my shoulder quickly and spot Leo looking this way while Camila accosts him.

Leo, tell Mack it's time to put our plan into motion, asap.

Leo shakes his head. ***Plan? This will not end well, Bizzy.***

It will, I assure him. ***And it ends now.***

Jasper follows my gaze and his jaw tightens. ***He's looking at Bizzy again. And this time, it feels as if she's looking right back. I hope it's nothing. But then, I've hoped that before.***

We head to Jasper's cottage, and I try to show him exactly how devoted I am to him.

Soon enough, Camila won't be a problem and we can get right back on track, where we belong.

16

The Country Cottage Inn plays host to a number of events all year round, and the most elegant of them all is tonight's annual charity event run by the city council. The Let It Snow Ball promises to be absolutely opulent. I hope.

As the manager of the inn, it's my responsibility to keep the Christmas magic alive, and it's a bit harder to do with a woman ranting and raving as she schleps a bevy of quilted duffle bags down the stairs.

To my surprise and somewhat delight, the ranting and raving lunatic is the exact ranting and raving lunatic I was hoping it would be—Camila.

Fish stands on the counter, and the hair on her back rises an inch. ***Here comes trouble.***

Mistletoe and Holly give a lazy glance toward the commotion.

Mistletoe yawns. ***As long as we're not spending the night in the trunk of her car, we don't care where that woman goes.***

Both Grady and Nessa, my trusty employees, run to aid Camila in the effort before she chips a nail, or cracks her skull open and sues the inn, or worse yet, me.

Mackenzie crops up with her shoulders back, a dark smile cresting her lips as we witness the spectacle.

I lean in toward Mack, never taking my eyes off Camila. "How did you pull this off so quickly?"

The queen of chaos barrels over before Mack can answer.

Camila's hair is slightly disheveled, her mascara runs down one side, and she looks as if she got dressed in the dark.

She grunts at the two of us, "Don't you think for a minute this is over."

"Oh?" Mackenzie pulls out her phone. "Maybe I should place that call to the district now?"

I suck in a quick breath. "Oh goodness, Mack, please tell me that's not what you threatened her with." I cringe at the thought of Mackenzie finding out about that awful calendar. I feel terrible for hinting at the fact I knew something to begin with.

"What else would the two of you threaten me with?" Camila all but rips the phone out of Mackenzie's hand.

I press my hand to my chest. "Camila, I'm so sorry. I never meant to let it slip."

"Of course, you did." A short-lived smile twitches on her lips "And I'll go." She blows out a quick breath as her eyes meet up with mine. "I take it the maniacal mayor doesn't know the secret you and Leo are keeping, does she?"

My stomach drops as I shake my head at Mack. "There is no secret. She's trying to manipulate you."

"Am I?" Camila chortles as if she caught her evil second wind. "Come now, both Jasper and Mayor Woods are smart people. They'll figure it out soon enough. And I'll be there to rescue Jasper in the fallout, fair and square." She glowers over at Mack. "And I just might take Leo back, too. I'm familiar with his type, Mayor Woods, and it's not you." She storms out of the inn, and poor Grady and Nessa follow along, rolling her endless parade of suitcases and bags.

Jasper walks through the door with a quizzical look on his face, glancing back at the spectacle Camila is making as she slogs off into the snow. Sherlock comes in bounding by his side, and I'd swear that he looks as if he's grinning ear to floppy ear.

It's over, Bizzy! You did it! You kicked her out. Sherlock lets out a bark in her wake. ***That's the best Christmas present you could have ever given me—and Jasper.***

Mackenzie presses her hand to my chest. "If I find out there's something funny happening with you and Leo, you are next on my hit list, Bizzy Baker." She takes off as Fish hisses and does her best to swipe at her.

"Bizzy Baker"— Jasper opens his arms and I head right over to fill them—"it looks as if Christmas came early. Who do I have to thank for that?"

"Camila Ryder, herself." And her poor decision-making skills. "Anything new with the case?"

He winces. "It was oleander in that toxin, all right. But oleander and antifreeze are just about everywhere you look in this town. It's not quite the smoking gun you'd think it would be."

"That's too bad." I glance back to my purse lying behind the counter. "Jasper, I may have something that could peg the Bronsons with Lincoln's death—or at least one of them."

He leans in, trying to hook my gaze. "What is it?"

My mouth opens and all sorts of sounds croak out. “Okay, I might have procured a bottle of that proprietary blend antifreeze Dexter sells at his shop.”

His hold loosens on me as he searches my features. “Wait. Dexter Bronson sells a proprietary blend of antifreeze at his shop?”

I give a quick nod. “I think it’s exclusive to him.”

“Exclusive, huh?” ***I’d better get out there.***

“Oh, you don’t have to.” I suck in a quick breath because, holy stars above Cider Cove, I just answered his thoughts.

I cringe. “Wait here.” I pick up my purse and head right back. “I just so happen to have a bottle.” I reach in and pull out the svelte blue plastic container, holding it out as if it had the power to gleam all on its own.

“Bizzy?” He tips his head to the side. “When did you get this? Did you go to Edison? Please tell me you didn’t talk to Dexter Bronson. Somebody who is willing to poison someone is a loose cannon.”

“Yes and no.” I duck a little. “I swiped it from his garage.”

“Bizzy, you”—he glances around and walks us away from a small crowd that just bustled through the door—“you stole this? What’s gotten into you?”

My mouth opens and closes. “Leo encouraged me to do it.” Okay, so throwing Leo under the bus wasn’t most likely the best move on my part for several obvious reasons.

“*Leo*?” His whole body stiffens in a silent rage. “Bizzy, what is going on between the two of you?”

“Nothing, I swear.”

“I’m beginning to think it’s something.” He glances to the bottle in his hand. “I’m going to make a few calls and try to get this tested as soon as possible. Would you watch Sherlock for me?”

I give an eager nod.

“Great. I’ll see you tonight, Bizzy.”

Jasper storms off, bottle in hand, and I give Sherlock a quick scratch between the ears.

I hope whoever killed Lincoln Bronson didn’t just kill something else—namely my relationship.

I shake my head at the thought.

Camila is gone, one or both of the Bronsons will be behind bars soon enough, and Jasper and I are going to get right back on track.

I hope.

17

The Let It Snow Christmas benefit is just getting underway as I stand at the reception counter welcoming all of the elegant women and the dapper men by their sides.

The mistletoe is hung—thanks to Georgie and her amorous frame of mind—and the trees are lit and sparkling like jewels adorned with dozens of red ornaments and big red velvet bows. Two oversized wreaths hang over the entry to the inn, and they're both lit with hundreds of twinkle lights. Jordy worked hard all month hanging garland around the entire periphery of the building outside, and because we've had a fresh snowfall all day, he even built a snowman for us out front. It's unusual for us to get snow around coastal Maine even in December, but it does happen and I'm thrilled to pieces it's happening tonight because it's simply magical.

Of course, I'm not leaving my menagerie out of the festivities. I put a bright red velvet bow on all the pets tonight. Fish sits proudly on the counter next to Mistletoe and Holly, and the three of them look like a trio of cute little gifts that Santa dropped off early. With their fluffy black and white striped fur, the three of them are starting to look like sisters now that the younger kittens have filled out a bit.

Sherlock has a plaid red bowtie on, along with those cute antlers we picked up last night, and not a single person has been able to resist him.

Nessa comes over in her glittering navy gown. Nessa Crosby looks like a supermodel in whatever she decides to throw on, but tonight she looks like a goddess.

"Go on, Bizzy." She shoos me off with her hands. "You can check out the auction items now. I've already bid on six different things. They have a cabin available for three nights at the Windy Pines Lodge, and if I win I'm going to need a few days off."

"If you win, I'll be more than happy to give them to you."

"Good luck!" she calls after me as I head into the brightly lit ballroom with its chandeliers glittering above like diamonds on a moonlit night.

It's wall-to-wall people in here, and every face is a familiar one. All of Cider Cove has come out to help the needy families in our area. There's a large tree in the center of the room, and an entire crowd of people is trying to take a picture of its splendor. It's the only tree in the inn that's flocked and looks as if it's just been doused with sparkling pink snow. It's a wonder all on its own, and I'm half-tempted to take a picture of it myself when I spot my father heading this way, a huge grin on his face that never seems to leave.

"Bizzy Bizzy!" He pulls me in for a quick embrace. He's donned a nifty looking dark suit and looks as dashing as can be. "You pulled it off. The place looks great, kiddo. And so do you."

"Thank you," I say, glancing down at the red velvet dress I salvaged from a vintage shop down the street. It's off the shoulders and formfitting up top with a bell skirt. I just had to have it once I saw it. "So where's the lucky bride-to-be?" I crane my neck past him, but I don't see a trace of Jasper's mother.

"She's around somewhere. We ran into Ree, and you know how your mother is. She insisted on having a quick chat with her."

My mouth falls open. "With Gwyneth? And you didn't protest?"

He shrugs as if it were no big deal. "They're grown women. What's the worst that could happen?"

"Garland could be used as a strangulation device—against *you* once Mom spills the dirt she's been acquiring on you for years."

He belts out a laugh before stopping abruptly. "On second thought, I'd better go hunt them down."

Georgie runs my way before I can make a move. She's donned a red glittering kaftan and has a wreath of gold garland in her hair, giving her that seventies flower child vibe and I love it.

"Bizzy Baker, I just bid on the muffin basket of the month from the Country Cottage Café."

"Georgie, you could have all the muffins you like, year-round for free," I whisper, lest another guest should hear me. Georgie might have a few more perks than other guests, but that's because she's one of my favorite people on the planet.

Her eyes narrow in on mine. "Rub it in my face, why don't you." She gives a little wink. "I'll be sure to pass on the freebies to Maurice if I win."

"Who's Maurice?"

"My favorite bartending hot buttered bun, if you know what I mean. Speaking of which, I'd better track him down before he melts away." She zips off, and I spot Calvin by one of the many auction tables.

Calvin St. James wanders slowly with his arms folded across his chest as he inspects the long line of wares up for grabs. There are baskets filled with books, and cooking supplies, one with sports memorabilia, and a few with gifts that are already wrapped for both men and women. Calvin looks smart in a dark suit and bright green tie. His thick hair is combed back, and yet he looks stoic at the surroundings as if he were waiting for it all to be over with.

"Calvin," I say as I stride right up to him. "Can I offer you a refreshment? We've got hot cocoa and hot apple cider, and, of course, regular coffee and peppermint mocha, too."

"That's okay, Bizzy." He perks up just a bit. "I'm just waiting for my girlfriend to get a good look around."

"How about you? Are you bidding on anything?"

"Not tonight. And maybe not ever again. They just had the reading of Lincoln Bronson's will, and I'm up a creek without the financial paddle I thought I'd have." He blows out a breath. "When you work your whole life only to meet up with a crooked business partner, it's a bitter pill to swallow."

"I'm so sorry. I thought Lincoln Bronson was sitting on an entire pile of money."

"I did, too. But as of late, it seems to have up and disappeared. If you'll excuse me, I think I'll have that peppermint coffee now and I'd better track down my date." He takes off, and I blow out a breath after him.

I think Calvin St. James might just have the toughest pieces to pick up after Lincoln's death.

No sooner do I have the thought than I spot both Mary Beth and Dexter Bronson. Gone is Dexter's Santa suit and in its place is a bright red tuxedo. At least he has no problem standing out. Something tells me he enjoys the attention. Mary Beth is wearing a dark green drape that I'm not sure if it's an actual dress or an ill-fitted poncho.

Mary Beth spots me and waves. "*Bizzy*." She scuttles this way. Her dark hair looks freshly dyed and her nails are bright red and sharpened like daggers. "I just have to win that basket full of jams and jellies." She leans in and the scent of her musky perfume makes my eyes water. "I'm the head of the parent-teacher association down at Cider Cove

Elementary and we would love to make a donation on behalf of the PTA."

"That's so nice of you." I inch back to get a better look at her. Are killers always this nice? Maybe she's trying to throw me off her scent. "How is everything going in the neighborhood?" I'm half-tempted to text Jasper and let him know our two prime suspects are standing right in front of me.

She glances back at Dexter before leaning in. "It turns out, Lincoln left me his house." She grimaces before tittering with a nervous laugh. "Can you believe it?"

"Wow, that's—well, I guess he thought very highly of you."

She shrugs. "At first I was baffled by it, but it's official. He filed with his attorney just a few weeks back." She shudders. ***If that doesn't make me look like the killer, I don't know what does. If I didn't know better, I'd think someone were trying to frame me.***

The killer? As in not her?

I glance to Dexter as he finishes bidding on a signed basketball.

"Well, congratulations on that. I mean, you did gain something very valuable."

Dexter pops up behind her and raises a mug of hot cider my way. "It's the cookie girl. Did Mary Beth tell you the news? It's like we won the lottery." ***Except my wife had to sleep with her ex to get the prize.***

"Yes, she did," I say. "In fact, I was just congratulating her. What do you think you're going to do with it?"

"Burn it," Dexter deadpans, inspiring Mary Beth to honk out a laugh.

She leans in. "I'm going to spruce it up and see if I can't get a mint out of it when it goes on the market this spring. Who knew it would be Lincoln Brooks who would put my kids through college?"

Dexter smacks his lips as if the idea didn't sit well with someone else providing for his family.

He lifts his drink once again. "You know what they say—easy come, easy go. I might use it as a man cave until then."

Mary Beth grunts, "Good luck getting Julia to leave."

"Oh, she is leaving," I volunteer. "She got a job down in South Carolina. She's leaving on Monday."

"Monday?" Mary Beth presses a hand to her chest. "Christmas Day?" She shudders dramatically and belts out a groan along with it. "You couldn't pay me to travel anywhere that day, or about a week afterwards. It's odd, don't you think? No family, no friends. She's just worked for Lincoln for about eleven months."

"That's too bad. I think she liked him and would have stayed longer if she could have."

Dexter lifts his brows as he turns away. ***She liked him, all right. A little too much. I will never understand the spell Lincoln Brooks cast on women.***

I look to Mary Beth. "Do you know where she's from originally?"

"Kansas?" She points to the ceiling. "No, that's not right. Texas, maybe? Anyway, I know for a fact she said she worked in New Hampshire just before this."

"It sounds as if she moves around a lot." Poor thing. It must be near impossible to develop healthy relationships that way. No wonder she appreciated the attention Lincoln was giving her—inappropriate as it was. If it's true at all.

But I would have killed him if he tried to pull a move on me.

A cold shiver runs through me just as my phone pings.

"Excuse me," I say as I step away from Mary Beth and Dexter. "Please be sure to snatch up some gingerbread whoopie pies at the refreshment table. They're baked fresh right here at the inn." I glance down to my phone to see it's a text from Jasper, and I quickly head for the exit as I read it.

It's a match. The concentration of methanol was unique to that product. Bizzy, if you see either one of the Bronsons, I'm asking you to steer clear. I'm on my way to the inn. See you soon.

"Oh my goodness." My heart thumps into my throat as I turn around and spot the two of them not only happily noshing away on my gingerbread whoopie pies, but stuffing their pockets with them, too.

Perfect. They're killers *and* they're thieves. Although I'm not sure loading up on free carbs is stealing, but nevertheless.

I turn to leave and nearly knock over the woman in front of me. I stabilize her by the arms and she laughs.

"Hello to you, too, Bizzy."

"Julia." I breathe a sigh of relief.

She has her hair swept back into its signature bun, and she's donned a plain black dress.

I'm half-tempted to blurt out everything to her regarding what Jasper discovered, but I decide to keep it close to the vest for now. "I'm glad you're here. I know you're leaving soon, but most of the items up for auction are ready to take home tonight."

She shakes her head. "I just came to say goodbye. I actually buttoned up everything earlier today. My car is all packed, and I'm leaving tonight. I'm driving down to

McBride and spending the night. I'll drive down as far as I can get the next day. But I'll check out the auction items anyway. Who knows? I might just find something I can't live without."

My expression sours just hearing the news. "I'm really sorry to see you go. I just wish I had met you sooner. We could have been great friends."

"I think we're great friends already." She glances past me and makes a face. "I see they're here. I'm shocked they haven't been arrested yet." ***Nothing burns me more than to see those two enjoying the holidays. They should've been locked up by now. One of them at least.***

I can't say I blame her for thinking it. But it is the holidays and the Bronsons have children. This might very well be the last Christmas they spend as a family for a very long time.

Julia shakes her head. ***With all the clues out there, you'd think connecting the dots wouldn't be all that hard.***

I nod without meaning to. "You know, with all the clues out there, you'd think those two would be behind bars by now." I know I shouldn't echo people's thoughts, but it was far too tempting.

Her mouth rounds out as she smiles. "That's funny. I was just thinking the same thing. I knew I liked you."

"So, what's your new gig?" I ask. "You're not doing time in a B&B again, are you?"

A laugh bubbles from her. "Nope. It's another older gentleman. He needs someone to manage his finances while he goes off wine tasting and fox hunting." She rolls her eyes.

"Another older gentleman?" I tease. "I'm beginning to think you have a type."

"I'm beginning to think you're right."

"Good luck winning those auctions," I say. "They can be cutthroat, especially this time of year."

"Don't worry about me, Bizzy. I've cut a proverbial throat or two. Besides, I do some of my best work this time of year."

We share a warm laugh as she excuses herself to peruse the offerings.

I head back out into the main hall and spot a woman with a long blonde ponytail and lashes the size of that evergreen back in the ballroom.

"Trixie! I'm so glad you could make it. I just ran into Julia in there. It's her last night. She's leaving town right after this."

"Leaving town?" She smirks. "I suppose she got a piece of the Lincoln liar pie, too."

"I don't think so. She didn't mention it."

"Please, Bizzy." She takes a moment to fan her ponytail over her shoulder. "It's always the quiet ones you need to look out for." She takes off, but her words resonate in my mind.

Julia is definitely a quiet one, but only because she's sane and stable. She worked at a B&B once, for Pete's sake. We're in the same line of work, or at least we were. It's no wonder I've taken such an instant liking to her.

What did she say the name of that B&B was? I forgot to ask her why she left in the first place. Although I could probably come up with a dozen reasons off the top of my head. Dealing with the general public isn't always easy.

I think back on it. East West Inn? No, that's not right. West River Inn? Oak Falls B&B! That's what it is.

I pull out my phone and do a quick search of it. I can't help but feel a little competitive with other inns and bed and breakfasts. In my mind, there is no other place quite like this one.

A bevy of articles pops up regarding the Oak Falls B&B, and I glance at all the headlines in horror.

What? I shake my head at the phone.

A million thoughts crash through my mind all at once.

"Nessa?" I say as I speed over to the counter and snatch up my purse. "I'm going to step out for just a second. I left an old box of books in the back of my car."

Sherlock perks right up and shakes out his fur as if he were coming out of hibernation.

I'm going with you, Bizzy.

Fish yowls, ***I'm not. I hate snow. It's cold and it makes my paws glide out from under me. Don't fall, Bizzy. I hear they put the cone of shame on people, too.***

Nessa comes around the counter as if she were chasing me. "And you need those books *now*?"

"Yes, I do! I'm parked right outside," I shout as I run out the door and into the snow that's coming down in a flurry. Usually, I leave my car in the driveway of my cottage, but tonight I was hauling over a few things for the auction and I happened to park in the lot just a few rows over to the left. This should only take a second.

It's so cold out.

Snowflakes fall over my bare shoulders, and each one feels like the bite of a flame.

I make a beeline for the trunk of my sedan and quickly pop it open. There's a streetlamp up above, and it exposes that box full of books as if they were sitting in the afternoon sun.

I pick up the one on top, *The Necrotic Botanist*, and begin flipping pages.

Something Calvin said comes back to me. He said the killer was smart to do this during a season with so many diversions.

Julia's words rush at me in a flurry. *"Don't worry about me, Bizzy. I've cut a proverbial throat or two. Besides, I do some of my best work this time of year."*

I stumble upon a dog-eared page in the book I'm holding and bring it close to read the chapter heading.

Oleander, the Deadliest Bush of Them All.

And just like that, I know who killed Lincoln Brooks.

18

“Bizzy?”

I glance up to see Julia Hart with her arms loaded with a basket of jams and jellies. I’m sure Mary Beth won’t be too happy about not winning that auction. But then, she might be a little more upset if she knew the seemingly sweet girl before me is trying to set her up for a murder wrap. That is, if I’m right.

Lincoln Brooks had a lot of money, and nobody knows where it went.

And the one that was in charge of Lincoln Brooks’ affairs just so happens to be leaving town.

Sherlock moans as his antlers blink on and off like a seizure. ***I don’t like this, Bizzy. Let’s get back inside.***

"Julia." I close the book and glide it behind my back as I drop it into the trunk.

Her eyes trace my every move as she steps in close. "What do you have there?" She cranes her neck a bit. "Oh, a book." She gives a little laugh until she sees it for what it is and clears her throat. "This basket is getting heavy. I slipped the girl a wad of cash and she let me take it early." ***I knew I wanted this basket of glorified sugar as soon as I saw Mary Beth circling around it.***

"That was good thinking." I have a feeling Julia is very crafty when it comes to getting what she wants. "Here, let me help you," I say as I shut my trunk, taking the heavy basket from her. "Wow, this weighs as much as a refrigerator."

A dull laugh strums from her. "Funny you should say that. It will be my pantry for the next week as I drive down to South Carolina."

That older gentleman she's headed off to work for bounces through my mind, and my heart seizes when I think of what might come of him.

"My car is right there." She points to a dark hatchback parked in a secluded area of the lot. "I'll pop the trunk."

"So, Julia, please tell me the name of the town you're headed off to. I have an aunt in Charleston I visit each January, and I would love to grab lunch with you if I can."

I don't have an aunt in Charleston, but I'm not sure the truth matters anymore in our short-lived friendship. I have a feeling it was all built on lies.

She glances my way as she pops the trunk. "You want to know the name of the town?" She reaches over and takes the basket from me before setting it down with a thud. "So you could visit?" She pulls something out from the back of the trunk, and before I know it, I'm staring at the barrel of a gun. "Or is it so you can rat me out to that ridiculous boyfriend of yours?"

Sherlock lets out a sharp bark. ***Nobody calls Jasper ridiculous but me. Now let's get inside, Bizzy. My paws are beginning to freeze.***

My hands slowly rise despite the fact she didn't instruct me to do it.

Bizzy? Sherlock growls. ***What's happening? Why does she have the no-no that Jasper keeps out of my reach?***

That no-no happens to look just like the Glock Jasper carries.

"Julia, you don't have to do this. I'll go back to the inn, and you can drive away."

A dull laugh expels from her. "Right. So you can make a few calls and the sheriff's department can intercept me? I don't think so. I'm afraid you're going to have to come with me." She gives a little shrug as she raises the gun up a notch as if sharpening her aim. "But, of course, I can't take you alive. I find it much easier dealing with bodies." A tight smile rubber bands across her face. "Try not to muck up my basket of jams and jellies with your blood." ***It looks as if I'll be switching cars and identities sooner than I thought.***

"You killed Lincoln." The words pant from me in a white frozen plume.

A killer? Sherlock gives a sharp bark.

"Shut up or I'll kill you first," she bleats his way.

A dull huff comes from me. "And you set up Mary Beth and Dexter because they were easy suspects. You used their oleander bushes and the antifreeze from Dexter's garage."

A sharp laugh belts from her. "Don't forget our dear friend Trixie. She had a motive, too. She was the one I was initially going to put all of my energy in, but once I found out about the affair Mary Beth and Lincoln were having, I thought, why not take down a marriage in the process?"

"And a family."

"They weren't a good one," she shoots back.

"That's not for you to decide, Julia. I did a little digging on the Oak Falls B&B. You killed your boss. You poisoned that poor man, too, didn't you? And you made sure to do it during everyone's favorite time of year because most people are too busy to notice a well-orchestrated murder. I see you framed his ex-wife as well."

Sherlock barks up a storm. ***You really told her, Bizzy. Can we leave now? I'll push her in the snow and you can run.***

Julia's eyes widen a notch. "You did your homework, didn't you, Bizzy?"

"Not soon enough."

Her features harden over mine. "If I knew better, I would have framed your mother."

I nod to the eager pup at my side. "Sherlock, *now*!"

He lunges for her and sends her plunging backward. The gun goes off like a violent clap of thunder, and without thinking, I dive for it.

"No!" Julia cries as she tries to wrestle me away. "I'm sorry, Bizzy. You shouldn't have put your nose where it doesn't belong." She grunts as she pushes me back a good three feet and I glide over the snow. "But I can't let you go. You know too much."

Sherlock jumps and barks into the night as Julia and I push and pull at one another's limbs.

"Why kill those poor men? Why not just take their money and run?" I grunt right back as I struggle to get past her.

"Death is the only way two people can keep a secret, Bizzy. It's the only way you'll keep mine." Her hand slaps down over the gun, and a spear of defeat rides through me.

"Freeze!" a deep voice bellows from behind, but Julia snatches up the weapon regardless and I catch her wrist before she can point it at me.

A body falls over the two of us, and it's Jasper's face I see next to mine.

In a flash he has Julia's arms behind her back and Leo is right there to cuff her.

Jasper pulls me into his arms and helps me to my feet.

"Bizzy Baker." He buries a kiss into my hair as he holds me tightly. "You are going to be the end of me. Are you okay?"

"I'm fine. I promise." I pull back, panting. "She did it. She confessed. Julia killed Lincoln. And she killed her old boss, too, and who knows how many more people. She's a serial killer is what she is."

Julia grunts and groans as Leo leads her past us.

"That's right, Bizzy. I'm a killer." She tries to lunge at me as Leo holds her back. "And if I ever get out—and I will—I am going to hunt you down. I wouldn't sleep tight if I were you. I hope you live in fear for the rest of your life!" she roars out those last words at me and they echo through the night.

"Don't worry"—Jasper whispers as Leo leads her toward the bevy of patrol cars speeding to the scene—"you'll be sleeping safe. I'll make sure of it." ***In my arms if she'll let me.***

"You really do care for me, don't you?" A tiny smile cinches on my lips as I look up at this gorgeous man with silver eyes.

"I more than care for you." His chest expands as he presses his eyes to mine. "I love you, Bizzy."

A breath hitches in my throat as my mouth rounds out in wonder. "You just said you loved me." My entire body trembles with delight. "I love you, too, Jasper."

Snow falls a little quicker as Sherlock barks and jumps, this time with glee.

And in that microcosm of a second, all is right in the world—and in my heart.

Jasper and I share a kiss that says *I love you* without the use of words.

It looks as if it's going to be the merriest Christmas of them all.

19

Christmas Eve in Cider Cove is special every single year. But Christmas Eve in Cider Cove with *snow* is an extraordinary bliss.

All of Cider Cove has been turned into a virtual winter wonderland this afternoon and well into the evening. My dream of having an old-fashioned Christmas at the inn might have been usurped a teeny bit, but a wedding is always a welcome addition to a festive celebration.

All of the usual suspects are here—my mother, my sister, my brother, Georgie, and, of course, my father—Gwyneth and her children, Dalton, Jamison, Maximus, Ella and her husband, and best of all Jasper. Emmie, Jordy, and their parents have joined us, too. Gwyneth let us know Camila couldn't make it, citing she wasn't feeling well.

I've got to give it to Mackenzie. If she's an expert at anything, it's making people *sick*.

And last, but never least, Sherlock and Fish are fast asleep underneath the Christmas tree, along with Mistletoe and Holly. They were so worked up all afternoon about getting a special Christmas dinner that as soon as they gobbled every last bite, they fell into a comatose state.

In an odd turn of events, Gwyneth decided she didn't want the masses pouring in to witness the matrimonial debacle about to take place between her and my father. Instead, she's opted for something rather low-key. Very, very low-key.

I make my way over to Mom, Macy, and Georgie who stand by the crackling fire dressed in their Christmas Eve finery.

"Mom, what did you say to Gwyneth to diminish the crowds to the lowest common denominator? My goodness, we're lucky she invited Dad."

Georgie growls, "She wouldn't even let me invite Maurice." She folds her arms over her chest in one quick, aggressive move. "And before any of you ask, he's my favorite hot buttered bartender."

Macy takes a sip of her mistletoe-tini and nods. "Those are my favorite kind of bartenders, too."

Even though the wedding is a much smaller affair, Gwyneth still has an open bar—the only real taker being Macy—and the Country Cottage Café has still provided a sizeable buffet dinner guaranteed to please those who prefer either a surf or turf dinner.

Emmie and I made sure there were lots of gingerbread whoopie pies on hand for all to enjoy, and along with them plenty of hot cocoa, apple cider, and eggnog.

And speaking of eggnog, Julia Hart was arrested and formally booked for the death of Lincoln Brooks. In addition to that, Jasper informed me that the homicide investigation of Julia's previous employer will be reopened, and the woman who was already serving time for the infraction will be temporarily released until the new investigation yields its findings.

I already know what they'll discover. In an irony only her moniker could provide, Julia Hart, in fact, was deficient in that very thing, *heart*. She is a cold-blooded killer who would have carried on her carnage again and again until someone came along to stop her. And for what? Plain and simple. *Greed*.

I'm glad it's over. I'm glad no one else will die at her hands.

Mom gives a little wave in front of my face. "You're thinking about it again, aren't you?"

A heavy sigh expels from me. “Yes, I confess I am.”

Georgie scoffs. “That’s three killers in a row, Bizzy Baker. I think you have a knack to catch a killer. Have you thought of changing professions?”

“No way. I like managing the inn just fine. Besides, I’m hoping my sleuthing skills won’t be needed ever again. I’m ready for Cider Cove to return to its pre-homicidal state of innocence.”

Macy squawks out a laugh. “As if that were possible. Cider Cove is a killer’s paradise. And along with their own depraved minds, we’ll start drawing in people interested in death tours.”

Georgie nods as she holds up a crooked finger. “Morbid tourism. Now you’re thinking, sister.”

“No, that’s terrible. We don’t want any of it.” I’m quick to refute it. “And I seriously doubt there will be any more killers here in Cider Cove.”

“I agree,” a deep voice strums from behind as Jasper wraps his arms around me. “I’m pretty sure Bizzy has scared them all off.”

A warm laugh breaks out.

I bat my lashes up at him playfully. “As long as I don’t scare you off, Detective.”

“I don’t think there’s a single thing you can do to make that happen. I promise it’s virtually impossible.”

The sound of a bell chiming goes off, and we turn to find Dad and Gwyneth standing by the oversized Christmas tree strewn with hundreds of white twinkle lights, so bright and shiny it's hard to see the ornaments through their luminescent blaze.

I look up at Jasper and try not to grimace or scream.

"It looks like it's time," I whisper.

Jasper closes those glowing gray eyes, and it's as if all the light goes out in the room.

"I guess it is." He sighs as he leads us in that direction.

Everyone gathers around the enormous evergreen as a justice of the peace that Gwyneth procured stands front and center.

Georgie elbows me in the rib. "I offered to officiate the ceremony, but Miss High and Mighty wouldn't have it." All eyes turn to my quirky, fun-loving friend and Gwyneth rolls her eyes. "I was too good for them anyway."

Macy leans in. "You can officiate my wedding, Georgie."

Mom belts out a laugh. "I wouldn't get too excited, Georgie. Macy has made it clear she's allergic to nuptials."

Macy scoffs. "That's because love is more than a piece of paper."

I lean over to Georgie. "You can officiate my wedding."

Jasper's chest rumbles with a silent laugh. "Mine, too."

"*Ooh*!" Georgie wiggles her fingers as if she were casting a spell. "Do you think it'll be the same one?"

A small round of laughter titters through the room.

Jasper offers a wry smile my way. ***It will be the same one.***

A visual of Leo and me at Candy Cane Lane bounces through his mind, and I cringe at the sight.

"It will definitely be the same one," I assure him and the room breaks out into a series of *oohs* and *ahs*.

Dad nods to the crowd. "Shall we begin?"

The mood shifts to something a touch more somber. This is a sacred event, and I can feel how special this is despite the fact I've lost count of how many wives my father has had.

Gwyneth shines in a winter white sparkling gown, encrusted with thick elegant beading, and I'm betting it weighs fifteen pounds at least. Her dark hair is pulled back into an elegant chignon, and her signature blood red lipstick looks less festive than it does dangerous.

"I have something to say." She flexes a short-lived smile at the small crowd of friends and family. She takes up both of my father's hands and looks lovingly into his eyes. "Nathan Baker, you are a prince among men. You are charming and wildly delightful and good in the sack, if I do say so myself."

A hard groan breaks out from the rest of us.

There are some things I can go a lifetime not knowing about my father, and that little coital tidbit is one of them.

"But." She tilts her head to the side. "After the rather enlightening and inspiring chat I had with Ree last night, I got to thinking."

And here we go.

I shoot my mother a glance, and she shrugs my way, a slight look of panic taking over her features.

Gwyneth nods to my father. "Nathan, I have decided that it's best we take things slow. I propose we report right back to this spot in exactly a year's time."

He jerks back as if she struck him. "You're calling off the wedding?"

"I'm calling *on* the engagement," she replies with a kind-hearted smile. "I've always wanted a long engagement, and you know what they say—there's no time like the present. This way, we can get to know one another a bit better. Ree is right. There's no need to rush down the aisle. It's not as if this is a shotgun wedding." She leans in close to him. "I've already had one of those."

A nervous titter of laughter circles the room.

Dad holds up one of Gwyneth's arms as if he were declaring victory.

"We're engaged!" he shouts with that signature grin of his, and the room breaks out into wild cheers.

Sherlock rouses to life and gives a few barks as Fish bounds over with the kittens in tow and I scoop the three of them up.

Mom takes the adorable tiny twosome from me. "Give me those sweet babies."

"You got it," I say, touching my nose to Holly's.

"No, I mean give them to me," Mom is quick to clarify. "I just can't stand the thought of these precious faces being without a good forever home. I'll take them both."

"What?" Georgie claps up a storm. "Now we've got a party!" She snaps her fingers and dances a jig.

"Mom, that's great," I say just as Hux and Macy come over. "Meet your new siblings," I tease.

Fish lets out a sharp meow of approval. ***If they're living with Grandma, that means I'll get to see them. And I'm glad about it, too.*** She juts her head their way. ***Merry Christmas, girls. You've found a wonderful home. And tonight I get the bed to myself again.*** She purrs as she looks up at me. ***You're still my favorite pillow, Bizzy.***

Macy coos at the two perfect angels. "They're the perfect crazy cat lady starter set. Congratulations, Mom."

Nessa walks in with her tiny mixed breed puppy with his black and white spots named Peanut. She adopted him last October after his owner was killed.

"Bizzy, there's a package in the lobby for you and Jasper. It sort of appeared out of nowhere." Nessa gasps as she looks from me to Jasper. "I didn't ruin some big surprise, did I?"

Jasper and I exchange a glance and shake our heads.

Jasper and I follow Nessa right back to the reception stand where she hands me a small red box tethered together with a black satin ribbon. I pick it up, and Jasper and I head over to the tree by the entry to open it.

"A gift to the both of us." I hold up the small red box no bigger than the palm of my hand. "Go ahead." I nudge it his way.

My blood runs cold as Jasper pulls back the ribbon and lifts the lid to the box right off it. Why do I get the feeling this gift is of a nefarious nature?

Inside sits a piece of paper, and Jasper quickly unfolds it and holds it out for the two of us to read together.

Dear Jasper,

You will have my undying affection until my last breath. What I'm about to tell you will be difficult to understand, but that won't stop me from looking out for your best interest, and the woman you've chosen to spend your time with certainly doesn't have your best interest at heart. She's keeping a dark secret from you. Bizzy Baker has supernatural abilities.

Don't believe me?

Ask Leo. He has them, too.

She may not be willing to tell you what they are, but I will.

Call me.

Yours forever,

Camila

It took far more fortitude than I have to resist from snatching that letter right out of his hand and tearing it apart, or *eating* it for that matter, so he could never tack the pieces back together.

But it's too late. He's read it.

The damage is done.

Camila's Christmas gift to the two of us is a dagger to the heart.

It just so happens that the dagger is also known as the truth, or at least as close as I'd like to get.

Jasper balks and laughs. "Okay, it's official. She's delusional. She's just trying to scare me off. Like I said, that would be impossible."

"We'd better call the men with the big nets." I force a dull laugh to evict from my throat, and it feels like a razor ripping its way out. "Would you like something to drink? I'm suddenly thirsty." I stagger over to the water dispenser near the reception counter and struggle to fill a paper cup because my hands are shaking so hard.

I'm stalling, buying time. How do I look into the eyes of the man I love and lie to him? Thankfully, he thinks Camila is desperate and reaching, and he's willing to laugh the whole thing off.

She *is* desperate and reaching, but right now that's beside the point.

Hello, are you Bizzy Baker? a deep voice calls from behind.

Great. A new guest. Maybe I can submerge myself in work for an hour and Jasper will forget all about that vindictive note.

"Yes, I'm Bizzy Baker," I call out, trying my hardest to compose myself as I take a moment to catch my breath. "How can I help you?" I ask without turning around. I can't face Jasper. Not yet.

My name is R.C. Kellogg. And I'd love a moment of your time to speak with you.

I pivot on my heels, and the smile glides right off my face. It's the two well-dressed men with dark hair and dark eyes who came by earlier this week—the men from the MRD.

Jasper's head tips to the side. "That was rather intuitive of you. They didn't say a word."

Bizzy Baker. The younger of the two nods my way. ***We'd like to have a word with you in private.***

I look to Jasper as his face bleeds of all color. It's as if he fully understands what's just happened, as if he's seeing me for the first time as the monster that I am, and I wonder if I've finally managed to do the impossible—scare him off for good.

Recipe

Country Cottage Café
Gingerbread Whoopie Pies

Hello friends! It's me, Bizzy Baker. As you may already know I'm a disaster in the kitchen, but lucky for the guests of the Country Cottage Inn, the Country Cottage Café has an amazing bakery that just so happens to have my best friend Emmie Crosby as the head baker. Emmie's Gingerbread Whoopie Pies are not to be missed this holiday season. It takes the spice of a gingerbread cookie, and the softness of cake, and combines them into one cream-filled delight. Trust me when I say these will be a treat at any holiday party or to simply enjoy for yourself. Happy holidays and happy baking!

Ingredients

2 cups all-purpose flour

2 teaspoon ground ginger

¼ teaspoon ground cloves

1 teaspoon cinnamon

1 teaspoon baking powder

1/4 teaspoon baking soda

1/2 teaspoon salt

1 egg

1/2 cup butter softened

1/4 cup brown sugar (pressed and packed)

1/2 cup evaporated milk

3/4 cup light molasses

1 teaspoon vanilla extract

1 teaspoon vinegar

Frosted Filling

1/2 cup unsalted butter, softened

3 ounces softened cream cheese

2 1/2 cups powdered sugar

1 teaspoon vanilla extract

2 cups marshmallow cream

2 tablespoons of milk

Instructions

Preheat oven to 350°

Add evaporated milk to vinegar and set aside.

In a mixing bowl, blend together flour, baking powder, baking soda, salt, ground ginger, ground cloves, and ground cinnamon.

In a large bowl combine butter and brown sugar. Cream together until light and fluffy. Whisk in the egg and molasses. Combine bowls of wet and dry ingredients. Add in milk and vinegar mixture, and vanilla extract, mixing thoroughly.

Drop one tablespoon of dough at a time onto a cookie sheet, spacing them about two inches apart.

Bake 10 -15 minutes until cakes are fluffy.

Cool to room temperature.

Filling

Blend cream cheese and butter until fluffy. Add vanilla and powdered sugar, blending with a mixer on high speed for 5 minutes. Stir in marshmallow cream. If mixture is heavy, add in 2 tablespoons of milk until light and fluffy.

Dollop filling between two cakes.

Serve and enjoy!

A Note from the Author

Thank YOU so much for coming along on this adventure with us! We hope you love Cider Cove as much as we do. We are SUPER excited to share the next book with you, BOW WOW BIG HOUSE (Country Cottage Mysteries 4)! Pooches reign supreme in the next installment, and so does murder. Thank you from the bottom of our hearts for taking this roller coaster ride with us. We cannot wait to take you on the next leg of the adventure.

Acknowledgements

A special thank you to the following people for taking care of this book—Kaila Eileen Turingan-Ramos, Kathryn Jacoby, Jodie Tarleton, Lisa Markson, and Ashley Marie Daniels. And a very big shout out to Lou Harper for designing the world's best covers.

A heartfelt thank you to Paige Maroney Smith for being so amazing.

And last, but never least, thank you to Him who sits on the throne. Worthy is the Lamb! Glory and honor and power are yours. We owe you everything, Jesus.

About the Author

Bellamy Bloom

Bellamy Bloom is a ***USA TODAY*** bestselling author who writes cozy mysteries filled with humor, intrigue and a touch of the supernatural. When she's not writing up a murderous storm she's snuggled by the fire with her two precious pooches, chewing down her to-be-read pile and drinking copious amounts of coffee.

Visit her at:

www.authorbellamybloom.com

Addison Moore

Addison Moore is a ***New York Times*, *USA Today***, and ***Wall Street Journal*** bestselling author who writes mystery, psychological thrillers and romance. Her work has been featured in ***Cosmopolitan*** Magazine. Previously she worked as a therapist on a locked psychiatric unit for nearly a decade. She resides on the West Coast with her husband, four wonderful children, and two dogs where eats too much chocolate and stays up way too late. When she's not writing, she's reading. Addison's Celestra Series has been optioned for film by **20th Century Fox.**

Feel free to visit her at:

www.addisonmoore.com